# VIP

## I'm With the Band

# VIP
## I'm With the Band

By Jen Calonita

Illustrated by Kristen Gudsnuk

LITTLE, BROWN AND COMPANY
NEW YORK   BOSTON

Text copyright © 2015 by Jen Calonita
Illustrations copyright © 2015 by Kristen Gudsnuk
Text in excerpt from *VIP: Battle of the Bands* copyright © 2016 by Jen Calonita
Illustrations in excerpt from *VIP: Battle of the Bands* copyright © 2016 by Kristen Gudsnuk

Little, Brown and Company

Hachette Book Group
1290 Avenue of the Americas, New York, NY 10104
Visit us at lb-kids.com

Little, Brown and Company is a division of Hachette Book Group.
The Little, Brown name and logo are trademarks of Hachette Book Group, Inc.

The publisher is not responsible for websites (or their content) that are not owned by the publisher.

First Paperback Edition: July 2016
First published in hardcover in December 2015 by Little, Brown and Company

The Library of Congress has cataloged the hardcover edition as follows:

Calonita, Jen.
  I'm with the band / by Jen Calonita ; illustrated by Kristen Gudsnuk. — First edition.
    pages cm. — (VIP)
  Summary: "Twelve-year-old Mackenzie Lowell goes on the road with her favorite boy band when her mom gets a job as the band's tour manager"— Provided by publisher.
  ISBN 978-0-316-25972-9 (hc) — ISBN 978-0-316-25974-3 (ebook) [1. Bands (Music)—Fiction. 2. Popular music—Fiction. 3. Automobile travel—Fiction. 4. Mothers and daughters—Fiction.] I. Gudsnuk, Kristen, illustrator. II. Title. III. Title: I am with the band.
  PZ7.C1364Im 2016
  [Fic]—dc23

                                              2014046848

Paperback ISBN 978-0-316-25973-6

10 9 8 7 6 5 4 3 2 1

RRD-C

Printed in the United States of America

*For my aspiring author little cousin,*
*Haley Ingram*

*"I feel blue if I say 'I love you' and you falter.*
*Why do you turn and walk away?*
*My heart knew the moment that I saw you,*
*That I need you like a fish needs water!"*

Zander Welling was singing to me! ME! I stared happily into his big blue eyes. The same eyes that were known to make girls hyperventilate and pass out at his concerts. Wow, that smile of his was mesmerizing, too.

GAH, was I drooling?

Drooling would ruin the moment. How often does the gorgeous lead singer of a boy band sing to you while you're running along a beach together? Wait. What was he doing now? He just stopped singing, ran a hand through his curly brown hair, and said, "Mackenzie, will you—"

"STOP DAYDREAMING!" My best friend Scarlet poked me hard in the cheek. "You heard the DJ! Perfect Storm ticket giveaway in five!"

I can't help it if I daydream about Perfect Storm. A lot. The latest was brought on by the results of the paper fortune teller our other best friend, Iris, made this morning. On my turn I learned:

I'm marrying Zander Welling! YES!

We're having three kids! COOL!

We're going to live in Saint Lucia! (FYI: That's my favorite Caribbean island. It's also the only one Mom's taken me to.) EXCELLENT!

I'm going to be an orthodontist. Wait. WHAT?

That last part *had* to be a mistake. Scarlet is the one who is going to be an orthodontist. She wants to invent a way for kids to benefit from braces without actually having to get braces, which sounds good to me. And I don't even need braces.

Everyone knows I'm going to be an artist. Not to brag, but my friends and our art teacher, Mr. Capozzi, say I'm the best artist in seventh grade at Brookside Middle School. I'm always doodling in my journal, on the chalkboard wall in my room, or in notebooks during class. Someday I'm going to have my own comic-book series called *Mac Attack*. I've already started working on the first issue. It's about a girl rock band that fights crime between shows, and the lead singer is named Mac (named after me, Mackenzie). The girls wear matching sparkly silver tank tops and pink-and-green camou-flage pants that look cool onstage but are comfy offstage for fighting crime. I haven't shown my first issue to anyone yet. It's TOP SECRET, but my friends have seen loads of other stuff I've drawn, like album art. That's my other

3

dream—to design album covers, and PS need one for their first full-length disc. Heath Holland, one of the band members, just tweeted that their album is going to drop early next year. This is what I came up with for them:

# PERFECT STORM

Get it? A ship called the PS lost at sea in a massive storm? Look at those rain clouds I drew! Scarlet and Iris say Zander, Heath, and Kyle Beyer (Perfect Storm's other member) are going to love it when I show it to them. There's just one small problem:

I have to meet them first.

"*I feel blue,*" I sang out loud, thinking of my awesome Zander daydream again. (True PS fans know the lyrics even though the new song hasn't been released yet. The guys put a sneak-peek clip online of them singing it.)

"MAC!" Iris's brown eyes were as wild as that banshee in the way-too-scary movie we watched the other night at our sleepover. Her strawberry blond hair looked like it had been in an electrical socket—probably because Iris had been pulling her hair out all day over these tickets. "We're supposed to be listening for the call-in sign," she said tightly. "Z100 is giving away only one more pair of tickets this afternoon, so stop distracting me!"

Geez. This ticket business was getting to Iris. She was right, though. My Zander daydreams were for during social studies (the Revolutionary what?) or car rides with Mom when she was on one of those long work calls with a client who was having what she called "an identity crisis."

We had to win those Perfect Storm tickets for tomorrow night, because, to quote Scarlet:

I'D RATHER LOSE MY PHONE FOREVER THAN MISS SEEING PERFECT STORM LIVE!

Perfect Storm is worth losing your phone for. The guys in the band go together as perfectly as Nutella and frozen bananas.

Zander Welling is dreamy, and we love his falsetto voice, but he's also funny and a little quirky (he's afraid of escalators). Plus, he's got a big heart. He started the Wishing You Well charity, which grants private concerts for sick kids. Is that generous or what?

Scarlet says Heath Holland is the cutest because he's charming and has a killer smile like Thor (who is our favorite Avenger). But Heath's superpower is pranks. PS's rebel band member has dropped water balloons on his bandmates; drawn Sharpie mustaches on Mikey G., their super-intimidating bodyguard; and played practical jokes on fans with Nerf water guns.

Kyle Beyer is . . . well, Kyle. We don't know a lot about the Brit because he's so quiet, but he's cute, he plays guitar, and he's in Perfect Storm. What's not to love?

Someday Perfect Storm is going to take over the world, but right now a lot of people still don't know who they are. I feel sorry that those people have a Zanderless existence. They need to turn on Totally TV more often. Scarlet, Iris, and I love that channel because they play way more music videos than MTV. When Perfect Storm's EP came out, the channel named PS one of their Totally Awesome Bands to Watch. We were hooked from the moment we saw Zander sing the first line of "I Could Love You Forever." I guess other girls were, too, because the guys' followers doubled in a week! Now their singles are playing on the Totally TV satellite radio station, and their You-Tube channel is getting super popular thanks to some shout-outs from famous bands. According to Heath's Twitter feed, the guys have already been booked to open at eight concerts this winter. Tomorrow they are doing one for Z100 called Song Slam on Long Island, and that's what we're trying to get tickets for.

Since the nosebleed seats at Nassau Coliseum start at $250, and none of our parents were buying the "I will die if I am not at this show" argument, Iris, Scarlet, and I had turned my bedroom into a Perfect Storm command center to win tickets from the radio station.

So far it wasn't going very well.

Today Z100 was giving away tickets every hour till six PM. We had missed the eleven AM through three PM giveaways, since we were in school. (Mom almost burst into flames when I suggested staying home to have more chances to win.) We ran home right after the last bell rang, but we lost the four and five PM slots. Next up was six o'clock, the final giveaway of the day, and WE WERE NOT GOING TO LOSE AGAIN!

Iris had had her ear glued to the radio in my room for the last ten minutes. Scarlet had tweeted the band all day, saying we were three broke girls trying to win tickets (to make them feel bad and just give us some). And I was, um, daydreaming about Zander. But as soon as we heard the DJ tell people to call in, we sprang into action.

"Dial! Dial! Dial!" Scarlet screamed, sounding like Coach Riley does when she yells at us for walking the track in gym instead of running.

We hit our phones like our lives depended on it. I could tell Iris was nervous because she started to sing off-key, and Scarlet flipped out.

"No singing!" Scarlet screeched as her fingers kept hitting the redial button on her bedazzled cell phone. That girl is lightning fast, which works out well for the school softball team (and hopefully radio contests). Scarlet is the ace first baseman on the team . . . or is that first base-girl? "Your voice is distracting!" Scarlet can be testy when she is feeling competitive.

I looked at one of my Zander posters that decorate my bedroom walls like wallpaper. "Can you believe she talks to her best friends like that?" I asked poster-Zander. I talk to my PS posters a lot, which may sound weird, but that's what happens when you're an only child and your mom works at a big tour management firm in New York City. She used to go out on the road with some of the biggest bands in the world, but when she had me, she took a job that kept her closer to home. Technically. Mom still works a lot.

"Mac, are you dialing or talking to Z. again?" Iris's voice was tense, too. Her fingers pounded angrily on her phone as well, and I winced.

"Yes, I'm . . ." I heard the busy signal stop and the phone begin to ring through. "It's ringing!"

The girls jumped up from their command posts—Scarlet on my bed, Iris in my beanbag chair, which was decorated with PS pillows we'd made.

"I knew your lucky charms would work!" Iris sounded way happier than she had a minute ago.

"Me too," I said, because it was true. When some girl named Annalise Arnold from Hamilton, New Jersey, won the five o'clock pair instead of us, I knew we had to get in a PS frame of mind, the way Zander does before each show. He's so into signs that he won't allow anyone in green backstage! We decided to go all out because we needed Z100 to grant us TWO pairs of tickets instead of just the one, since there were three of us.

### MAC'S TOP FIVE* LUCKY CHARMS
### USED TO WIN PS TICKETS

*Five is Zander's favorite number.*

1. Paint yourself with body art like guys wear at football games. (Iris drew the letters **PS** on her right arm during the last

12

hour and painted her face red. It was sort of horror-movie creepy and yet cool at the same time.)

2. We also all changed into red from head to toe the minute we got home from school and painted our nails red. It's Zander's favorite color.

3. Eat only PS's favorite foods. I ran to 7-Eleven to buy Cheetos, Rice Krispies Treats, red Gatorade (Z.'s fave!), and carrots during one of the breaks.

4. We also got superstitious and threw out my mom's asparagus (sorry, Mom!). Z. hates green food, which is why we hid the guacamole and Mom's gross kale chips and picked all the green M&M'S out of the M&M'S jar in the kitchen (I can't reveal where they ended up).

5. Speak with a British accent for two reasons: (a) Everyone sounds cooler with one and (b) Kyle is from London (although

13

he speaks so little in videos that it's hard to tell if he has an accent).

We were cheering so loud I almost missed the DJ say, "We've got the hundredth caller on the line."

"SHHH," I told the girls. Then I got ready to give my best radio voice, which I'd been practicing in my head (you have a lot of time to think when you're in your room for hours).

"Hey there!" the DJ said on the radio and on my phone. "Who am I speaking with?"

I opened my mouth to answer, and the line went DEAD!

NOOOOOOOOO!

I screamed so loud, dogs on my block started barking. "They hung up on me!" I cried as some girl who claimed to be Zander's future wife screamed on the radio as she won OUR tickets. "I was disconnected!"

"NO!" Scarlet freaked out. "NO! NO! NO! I'm

calling the station. They can't do that to us! You were the hundredth caller!" Scarlet began redialing. Then I heard her say, all cranky, "customer service representative" to the automated service, getting mad like my mom does when she can't get a real person on the line.

Iris and I flopped down on my bed and stared at my ceiling, where a poster of the boys dressed in blue stared back at us sadly. "I can't believe we're not going." Iris's voice was wobbly.

"Me either," I croaked, and then we were both quiet for a bit (aside from Iris's sniffling) while Scarlet kept yelling "CUSTOMER SERVICE REPRESENTATIVE!" into her phone.

I noticed half of Iris's red paint had rubbed off her face and onto my PS pillowcase. I was too depressed to care. "I really thought we were going to win today," Iris whimpered.

"I did, too. I already told everyone we were going, even though we didn't have tickets yet," I said.

15

Scarlet collapsed on the bed next to us. "Z100 said I have no way of proving we were the hundredth caller. Let's face it. We're not going to the concert." She threw her head back, and now the three of us were lying across my bed. We couldn't even muster up the energy to sing along to "I Need You (Like a Fish Needs Water)" when it came on the radio a few minutes later.

How would I ever show Zander the album cover I drew if we didn't meet at the concert?

I was so miserable that I didn't hear the knock on my door at first.

"Mac? Can you open up?"

It was my mom. It took forever to take the ten steps to the door. When I opened it, Mom looked way happier than we did. And pretty, too, like she always does in her cool-mom jeans and a jacket with necklaces that aren't the cheap kind from Claire's. Mom gets mistaken for my babysitter all the time, which I secretly think she loves.

"Why do you guys lock the bedroom door when no one is home?" she asked us.

"Banshees," the three of us said at the same time.

Seriously, that banshee movie was scary.

Mom leaned on my door. "You girls look pretty miserable for a Friday."

"We didn't win Song Slam tickets, which means we won't be seeing Perfect Storm live," Iris told her, and then she burst into tears. Iris cries over commercials with babies and always at the movies, but this time her crying had meaning.

"I know, I know, the tickets were expensive," I huffed before Mom could say anything. Iris was crying hard now, and Scarlet, who is usually very Heath-like (i.e., acts tough), was hyperventilating and doing that stop-start crying thing. So of course I started to cry, too. I looked at Mom. SHE WAS LAUGHING AT US! I couldn't believe my mom was so cruel.

"Mom!" I cried angrily. "It's not funny! I love

PS more than I love to draw." She stopped laughing. "Okay, not true, but they are a close second."

"I'm laughing because you're crying over nothing," Mom said. "If I had gotten home a few minutes earlier, I could have saved you girls a meltdown." She pulled four tickets from her pocket and held them up like a crane game prize. "Want to take a guess what these are?"

Scarlet and Iris practically ran me over to get to the door. I held my breath. Could it be?

My mom held the tickets out of reach. "Stop crying, girls. You're going to Song Slam!"

We screamed so loud my mom held her ears. Cody, the husky next door, howled.

"And these aren't just any seats," Mom said. "How does fifth row center PLUS backstage passes work for you three?"

This time we screamed so loud I thought my windows would shatter.

MY MOM IS THE COOLEST MOM EVER! I tackled her with a big hug. Scarlet and Iris joined me in making a Mom sandwich.

"How did you get these?" I asked. "I thought you said no one at work could get them."

Her smile was sort of sneaky. "Rumor has it your band is getting so big they might wind up opening for Lemon Ade on her new tour." My eyes widened. "A bunch of people from my firm are going to check them out. I guess you should get your red T-shirts ready," Mom said.

"How do you know about Zander's birthday request?" I asked. That morning he had tweeted that everyone should wear red to the concert.

"I know more about PS than you think I do," she said cryptically.

You know what? I didn't care how she knew. All I cared about was that I WAS GOING TO MEET ZANDER WELLING!

Who am I kidding? I can't sleep.

I'M MEETING ZANDER WELLING TODAY!

I can't decide which red shirt I am going to wear: the one I made on Tuesday with HAPPY BIRTHDAY, Z. written on a birth-day cake or the one I drew of the band for art class. Or maybe I should wear the one I did of their next album cover as designed by *moi*.

Decisions, decisions . . .

The most important one: What am I going to say to Zander when I meet him?

My opening line is key because I need those words to make Zander realize I am the only girl for him. Everything I've come up with, though, sounds lame ("It's about time we met!"), dorky ("I need you like a PS fan needs water!"), or stalker/creepy ("I'm a *perfect storm* of a girl for you, Zander!").

You know who wouldn't have trouble talking to Zander? My comic-book alter ego, Mac of the band Mac Attack. Comic-book Mac oozes confidence, while I leak nerves. If Mac Attack were going to the meet and greet instead of me, it would go something like this:

Sigh. I wish I was more like her in real life.

February 20th

**LOCATION:** *Home*

OH MY GOD, I STILL CAN'T BELIEVE WHAT HAPPENED TONIGHT!

Our concert experience started out the usual way—with Iris bugging out—but it ended like a scene from a movie!

"We'regoingtotouchZanderHeathandKyle andspeaktothem!" All of Iris's sentences sounded like one long word as we made our way through security at Nassau Coliseum. Iris sounded crazy, but she looked great. Her strawberry blond hair was straightened for the occasion, and her tan face was shimmery thanks to this cool glittery moisturizer she bought during an emergency trip to the mall this morning.

Scarlet had curled her black locks and used eyeliner to write "PS, We Love You" all over her right cheek and up and down her arms. Her face was flush, but it wasn't from blush. I think she was stressed. She was breathing into a paper bag as we scanned our tickets at the door and walked to the concession stand.

"What if I freeze up when Heath talks to me?" Scarlet asked us. She burst into tears, and my mom looked at her strangely. "I'm sorry, I'm just soooooooooo happy! I need at least ten photos, Ms. L., okay? Promise you'll keep snapping till someone forces you to stop. I need to get a good picture for this year's Christmas card."

Mom dabbed Scarlet's forehead with a cold water we'd just paid $4.50 for. (Concert food is such a rip-off!) "Girls, I've met a lot of musicians through my job, and the best thing you can do when you meet them is act NORMAL."

30

I knew Mom was right. She's taken me back-stage at concerts in New York City, and she always says the less you gush over artists, the more they'll talk to you.

"They want to be seen like everyone else." Mom stopped talking to read a text, then frowned. "Well, you guys can hold off on the PS meltdowns for a bit. They've moved the meet and greet to after the show. The guys were stuck in traffic and just got here a little while ago."

My stomach lurched like it does every time I go on a roller coaster at Hersheypark. Now I had two-plus hours to worry about what I was going to say to Zander. Z100 sponsored Song Slam, and, thankfully, we liked all the acts they had performing, so it was easy to get distracted. Hieroglyphics opened the show with fireworks, Banana Rama brought a fan onstage for their set, and then before I knew it, PS came on and did their set. Mom couldn't believe the fandemo-nium. They closed with a cover of the Beatles'

"P.S. I Love You," and I didn't even get annoyed when I heard the girl behind us ask, "Who are the Beatles?"

How could anyone not know the first—and most worshipped—boy band EVER?

The rest of the concert flew by. Lemon Ade played her new single, "Sour," and Mom even let me run out to the souvenir stand to get a new Perfect Storm T-shirt. I guess she's gotten over the time I came home with a seventy-five-dollar PS sweatshirt with Zander's face on the back. (She still doesn't know I wore it once before it shrank to the size of a Ziploc bag.) Then, a few hours later, it was really happening! The lights came up, I turned the lighter app off on my phone, and Mom was leading us to the side of the stage where a group of people was already waiting to meet PS. Scarlet screamed, "Look, it's Mikey G.!"

Mikey G., the band's bodyguard, was checking everyone in at the door, and he looked as mad as he does in pictures. He thrust a sticker at me that said SONG SLAM on it and VIP BACKSTAGE PASS written in Sharpie. I put it on proudly. I was going to frame that thing! Then we were walking down a hall backstage at Nassau Coliseum, which should have been exciting but was actually very anticlimactic. The halls were bland white and crowded with crates that roadies (as Mom calls them) kept dumping outlets, lights, and gear into. Mom said they were breaking down the "set," which is concertspeak for stage decorations.

"If you're here for Perfect Storm, come this way," called out a woman in a headset. We followed her into a big room, where there was a huge group of girls already waiting. Lots of adults in suits were standing around, and Mom walked over to some people from her firm. They started talking about how good PS's set was, but I didn't pay too much attention. I was on the lookout for Zander. I scanned the room and got momentarily distracted by a camera in my face. There were photographers everywhere taking pictures. Suddenly I began to feel very dizzy.

"Mac, you don't look so good." Iris put a hand on my back to steady me.

"Get in line for autographs, please!" A guy with a clipboard began nudging us forward. I felt like cattle. Through the crowd I could see the back wall, where there was a long table and . . .

Scarlet gasped. "IT'S PERFECT STORM!" The girls behind us started screaming.

"I never figured out my opening line," I mumbled to Iris. I pulled the T-shirts I had for the guys out of my bag. They were wrinkled like dirty laundry. Mom was too busy talking shop with work people to notice her only child was about to pass out.

"Smile, ladies!" one of the photographers said.

I fell flat like a pancake into a row of camera tripods and photographers, sending their camera equipment toppling like dominoes. The crash was deafening, like those fake ones you hear on cartoons. But it was all too real, and I lay on the floor, stunned.

"Mac!" Scarlet and Iris screamed. Mom tried to help me up, but I was tangled in wires.

"She broke my tripod!" one of the newspaper photographers complained.

"Is she all right?" I heard a man say. When he finally came into focus—things looked a bit hazy—I realized it was Briggs Pepper. He had a girl my age who looked like his daughter with him. A group started to form around us, and I heard someone ask if I needed first aid.

I was so mortified I wanted to die.

*Don't cry, Mac. Don't cry!* I told myself.

And then *he* appeared, and my whole night changed.

"Everyone back up. Give her some air!"

When he leaned down, I knew those sea-blue eyes right away. "Are you okay?" I managed a nod. Zander flashed me an ultrawhite smile and extended his hand. "Good. Well, let's get you up. I'm here to save you from yourself."

Melting!

THEN ZANDER WELLING HELPED ME UP AND LED ME THROUGH THE CROWD TO THE MEET-AND-GREET DESK!

Puddle on the floor!

Scarlet, Iris, and Mom hurried along behind me.

"Are you okay?" Zander asked me again as cameras clicked away. I saw a video camera zoom closer, too. "Ignore them and focus on me. What's your name?"

"Mac," I said, but it came out sort of garbled.

"Well, Mac, is that for me?" Zander pointed to the rolled-up shirts still in my hand. I held them out to him silently. "Thank you. Do you want to take a picture?"

I nodded.

"Guys, get over here."

Heath and Kyle were walking toward us! I could feel my heart pounding like a drum.

"Are those your friends?" Zander asked. "They can come, too." Scarlet and Iris ran over. I heard Scarlet squeak like a mouse when Heath put his arm around her. "Everyone smile!"

Mom took a bunch of pictures. Their photographer took a bunch of pictures. The cranky newspaper photographer whose tripod I broke took pictures. And I just stood there dazed as Zander turned to me and KISSED MY HAND!

"It was great meeting you, Mac. Thanks for coming," Zander said, and winked. Then he looked to the crowd. "Who's next? Oh, hey, Piper!"

Zander knew my mom?

"Nice T-shirt." I looked up. Heath pointed to the T-shirt I had decided to wear—it was a drawing of the guys' faces that I'd whipped up that morning when I couldn't decide between T-shirts. "Did you draw that?" I nodded, my eyes on his tattooed arms. Were they fake sleeves or real? I couldn't tell. "That's majorly cool, dude. Isn't that majorly cool, Kyle?" I didn't even notice Kyle standing there.

"Brilliant," Kyle said in his British accent, and then he smiled at me. Wow, he had nice eyes.

"I wish I had one of those," Heath said, and I couldn't help staring at his guyliner and the earring in the shape of a skull in his left ear.

"She made you each a shirt," Iris piped up as Scarlet hyperventilated. "Zander has them."

Heath grinned. "Awesome! Thanks!"

I looked over and realized Kyle was staring at me still. I could feel my cheeks redden. "Lovely to meet you, ladies," he said.

"Heath, Kyle, next group is waiting," Zander

said, and then the boys were gone before I could even explain my drawing.

But who cared?

ZANDER HAD KISSED MY HAND!

This was only the beginning, I was sure of it.

## Monday, February 22

I was too busy drawing to write yesterday. To be honest, I was also daydreaming about Zander. Did I mention that HE KISSED MY HAND? That has to be a sign that we're destined to be together.

Another sign: He posted a picture of a beach in the Caribbean on Twitter and wrote, "Wish I were here." We're meant to be! Well, as long as I can get over my fear of sharks. Scarlet and I watched *The Sharkinator Lives*, and after that I was scared of my own bathtub! In the movie a shark comes up the tub drainpipe!

SHUDDER!

But first things first: I had to make sure Zander didn't forget about me. The question was how. Sure, I could tweet Zander about our encounter, but I always gag when I read those kinds of tweets on his feed ("Remember me? You high-fived me during 'Love Bug' at the Wave One Winter Ball concert in Rochester, NY."). Not my style. If I was going to make an impression on Zander, I had to do something unique, just like Mac Attack would. In my comic, everyone remembers her because she fights crime with a metal nail file.

What is my secret weapon?

My art, of course!

Drawing is what I do best, and if I drew something that reminded Zander of how we met, then . . . well, then . . . then what? Even if he remembered me, it's not like he could invite me on tour. (How amazing would that be?) I needed to ask *him* to do something together, like . . .

(Long pause.)

Go to the Spring Fling!

The Spring Fling is going to be my first middle school dance, and everyone is talking about it already, even though it is still months away. Iris, who has two older sisters, says the dance is a make-or-break-you middle school rite of passage. Apparently, if you don't take a date to your first dance, then you'll be cursed to go to every middle school dance alone!

I cannot let that happen. I need to bring a date to the Spring Fling, and the only date I want to bring is Zander. So I got right to work and started to draw.

And draw and draw and draw and draw and draw and draw and draw and draw and draw!

I made several drafts of my poster before I finally had my masterpiece.

It turned out to be the best portrait of the band I've ever done. No, not just of the band, it's the best thing I've ever drawn, period! The

45

band is standing in the middle of my gym under a disco ball, but Zander is the star of the poster. I drew him standing in front of the guys, like he's going to pop off the page. Then I just had

to write him a note. I'm no Shakespeare, but I do know music—especially PS songs, so I used titles and lyrics from their album to write Zander's letter.

Zander,
I've caught the LOVE BUG! And it's all because of you. When I hear you sing, I NEED YOU, LIKE A FISH NEEDS WATER. And that's A GOOD THING TO FIND. So I have just one question, and the answer could CHANGE MY LIFE. My school has the DANCE OF OUR LIVES coming up, and I'd love nothing more than for you to be my date. It's in April, so we DON'T HAVE LONG TO WAIT. But I'll wait however long it takes to make you notice I'M THE ONE. WHAT DO YOU SAY, Zander? Will you BE MINE TONIGHT?

47

If my art teacher, Mr. Capozzi, saw this drawing, he would say, "You put some passion in your pencil!" It's his catchphrase, and thinking of him saying that made me a little sad. He was never going to grade this poster. What if my poster never made it to Zander, either? I had a sudden vision of my little poster collecting dust in a PS fan-mail bin for years, and I wanted to cry. My poster deserved better than that fate!

Then I had an idea: I quickly scribbled a note to the fan-mail peeps and stuck the sticky on the poster: "Please give this to Zander! If you can't, please send it back. This poster means a lot to me. Thanks!"

I signed it from Sabrina, which is my middle name.

My mom has a strict no-boyfriends policy for middle school ("You have high school and college for boys!"), so I didn't think she'd be thrilled about me asking a boy—let alone a celebrity boy—to the Spring Fling. And if PS mailed my art back, I definitely didn't want Mom opening my mail and reading my note to Zander. This way, Mom would think someone just had the wrong address and would set it aside.

I finally finished the poster when the sun was coming up this morning. Even though I was exhausted, I managed to create an e-mail address for "Sabrina" in case PS reached out. Then I carefully rolled the poster in a tube, addressed it to Zander care of the official PS fan club, rode my bike to the post office, and waited for it to open. The great thing about this being the first day of February school break is that I didn't have to wait until after school to send this message off to Zander. At 9:05 AM I wasn't in homeroom. I was at the post office making sure my poster was on its way! I had goose bumps when the postal worker stuck a FRAGILE sticker on the poster tube (at my insistence). If

49

Zander gets my message, I know he's going to flip over it.

When I came home, Mom was sitting at the kitchen table drinking her coffee with extra hazelnut creamer swirled into it. (She always tries to work from home a few days when I'm on school break.) "Where'd you head off to so early?" she asked with a yawn.

"Scarlet left her PS shirt here, and I wanted to get it back to her because it's her favorite," I lied, immediately feeling guilty. I was so excited about that poster that I wanted to burst! But I couldn't tell Mom.

"Why don't you have a seat? We need to talk about something important." Mom slid over a glass of chocolate milk. My favorite. Her mouth looked funny, and for a minute I got nervous. The last time she got like that was . . .

"Are we moving?" I blurted out. "I do not want to move to Los Angeles!" I freaked out. "I can't leave Scarlet and Iris or my school.

Mr. Capozzi is the best art teacher ever! Plus, PS are hardly ever on the West Coast. They spend all their time recording in New York and . . ."

"Mac?" Mom waved her hand in front of my face to get my attention "Calm down. We're not moving." She smirked. "Although we are going away for a month or two."

Just as my stomach started to settle, I felt it tighten again. "A *month or two*? Where are we going? How are we going away for so long? I have school."

"You're going to have a tutor," Mom said, and I opened my mouth to protest. A tutor? Did she mean homeschooling? "I don't think you'll mind the tutor at all, especially when you hear where we're going and *who* we're going with." She patted a manila envelope on the table. Intrigued, I sat down. "You're finally going to see Nashville, dip a toe in the ocean in Miami, ride a mechanical bull in Texas," Mom said excitedly. "All the things we talk about doing when they're doing them on *Life After Life*."

*Life After Life* is my mom's and my favorite soap opera. We DVR it every day and watch it together every night. The characters are always on the road. Mom and I talk about doing road trips like that all the time, but . . .

"I can't go away for months. I'll miss my friends too much. No sleepovers, no art class, no tae kwon do, no repeat viewings of *The Sharkinator Lives*."

"You hate that movie," Mom pointed out.

"Mom!" I was starting to get aggravated. I didn't understand what was going on. "We can't go away for more than a month! I have school and you have a job!"

Mom laughed. "Now you sound like the parent." She squeezed my hand. "Don't worry about my job. I'm going to be working the whole time." I must have looked confused because then she said, "Remember how you wanted to know how I got those PS tickets when no one could?" I nodded. "And how Zander knew my name backstage?"

I nodded slower and took a sip of my chocolate milk to calm myself down.

"It's because I've been meeting with Briggs Pepper the last few weeks, and he asked me to step in as PS's tour manager."

"WHAT?" I screamed so loud Mom's coffee shook. "You're going on the road with my band?"

Mom laughed. "We both are!"

My hands were shaking. My mom was going to be Perfect Storm's tour manager.

My mom was going on the road with Perfect Storm.

I was going on the road with Perfect Storm.

"How did this happen?" I asked, leaning in close so I didn't miss a word.

Mom explained that her firm had been talking to Briggs about how PS was blowing up. When PS was asked to open for the winter leg of Lemon Ade's Sweet and Sour Tour, Briggs decided to hire a tour manager to keep the band in line. Mom said she's known Briggs forever, since she went on the road with one of his other groups, and he immediately thought of her for this job. How did I not know they were friends? I could have met PS ages ago!

"I miss being on the road with a band, and

you and I have always wanted to travel, so this seemed like the perfect time to try tour life again," Mom said. "Briggs said PS has a bit of a reputation for playing practical jokes and making a mess of their greenroom at concerts, so he needs a tour manager to help keep them in line. Who better to do that than a mom?"

I pinched myself. *Wake up, Mac! Wake up, Mac!*

"You're not dreaming, Mac," Mom said. "We're going on the road with your favorite band. Traveling on the bus with them, staying at the same hotels, getting tutored together for school, having VIP backstage access at all their concerts. You are going to be hanging out with Zander, Heath, and Kyle 24-7."

That's when I let out such an ear-piercing scream that Cody the dog started howling and our neighbor Mrs. Greenbank called to make sure we weren't being robbed.

"THANK YOU!" I said, squeezing Mom like a lemon. "You're the best mom ever!"

Mom slipped something out of the envelope and over my head. "You're going to need this."

I looked down at the lanyard. There was a picture of PS on it, and on the back it said I'M WITH THE BAND: VIP ALL-ACCESS PASS FOR LEMON ADE/ PS TOUR.

Oh. My. God!

"You better get packing," Mom said. "We leave in two days for their first stop."

Two days till Zander and I are together for MONTHS!

# Wednesday, February 24

## LOCATION: Tour Stop #1—Atlanta, Georgia

When the pilot announced we were making our initial descent into Atlanta, my stomach dropped, and it had nothing to do with turbulence.

If we were approaching Atlanta, then that meant I was also approaching Zander, Heath, and Kyle.

Eighty-nine percent of my body was excited.

The other eleven percent was ready to throw up.

Mom getting this job with PS still feels like an amazing dream. I keep pinching myself to see if I'll wake up, but I don't, and now my arm is turning a nasty shade of purple.

As soon as we landed, Mom had to make a call to Briggs Pepper (who I assume I can soon call Briggs or BP or Briggsy, since we're going to be spending so much time together), and I got on the phone with Scarlet and Iris. Thankfully, they were together.

"You have to tell us EVERYTHING," Iris stressed. "Write it all down in the glittery diary we got you so you don't forget a single detail."

"I want to know what Zander's hair smells like, the sound of Heath's laugh, Zander's favorite subject in school—I can't believe you're technically going to school with Zander!" Scarlet was still freaking out. "Oh, and find out if Heath really wears guyliner. Maybe his eyelashes are just that amazing and it only looks like guyliner, you know?"

"Take lots of pictures with them," Iris added.

"And *draw* pictures, too," Scarlet said. "Being surrounded by such creative geniuses will make you think like a true artist."

"I promise. And I'll call you as much as I can. You know Mom limits my minutes."

"We know," they said together, sounding as dejected as I was at the thought of not talking to them at least four times a day. At home we practically lived together on weekends, and now I was being reduced to texts and occasional calls. When I complained, Mom suggested I send postcards from each city. Does Mom realize how long it takes a postcard to go through the mail? If I need to tell Scarlet what type of toothpaste Heath uses, I want to call her *right away*. Not three to five days from now. Who am I going to share all my Zander thoughts with 24-7?

"It's not like you're going to be gone forever," Iris said, sounding a little weepy. "You'll be back

61

before Spring Fling in April, and we'll all go together."

Spring Fling. With everything that had happened in the last forty-eight hours, I totally forgot to tell my friends about the poster I sent Zander asking him to the dance. But now I didn't need that poster at all. In less than an hour, I'd be able to ask Zander to the dance in person!

(Not that I had the nerve to do that. No. Way. I started feeling dizzy at the thought.)

I eyed Mom talking rapidly on her cell nearby. She noticed me and started waving me over frantically, like she was single-handedly trying to land a plane. "I should go," I said quickly.

I hung up and lunged for the pink, shiny suitcase that was spinning on the carousel toward me. The bag is decorated with my Sharpie drawings and artwork. Since we are going to be moving quickly from city to city, Mom told me to pack light, but try coming up with a ton of outfits to wow your favorite band when you only have room in one suitcase! Today I was wearing the same red T-shirt I had on at Song Slam. I was hoping Zander would remember it. As I pulled the bag off the belt, I fell backward.

A businessman on a cell phone helped both the bag and me to stand upright again. "Wow, that bag is heavy," the guy remarked. "Good luck carrying it."

Okay, maybe I had overpacked a little.

Mom rolled her small tan (or as I called it: boring) suitcase over to me with a frown. "I just spoke to Briggs," she said. "The boys were supposed to touch down in Atlanta last night, but their flight was canceled due to storms in the area, and they had to take their tour bus here. They've been on the road all night and will have to go straight to the radio interview they're doing this morning. We have to meet them there now."

"Right now?" I squeaked. No time to freshen up or spritz on vanilla body spray? (It smells like cookies, and Zander loves cookies.)

"Grab that bag and let's boogie." Mom took off at a near run.

I lagged behind, collapsing under the weight of my bag. I might have to ditch a few things, but that's okay. I'm sure all this time on the road has made PS expert travelers. I could just picture Zander and me packing our bags together at the hotel, him explaining to me the art of rolling

T-shirts and stuffing them in shoes to save room
and—

"Mac! Come on!" Mom yelled.

Not-so-fun fact about Atlanta: It's almost
impossible to—as Mom says—*boogie* (cringe).
The traffic is worse here than in New York. That's
what our cabdriver, Churro, told us when we sat
in gridlock for almost an hour to go someplace
that apparently should have been only twenty
minutes away. "The ATL is known for its beats
and its traffic, and you ladies are going to experience both today—if I ever get you to HotLanta
95.7," Churro said.

"From now on we'll be riding with the band,"
Mom told me through gritted teeth.

That was a relief. Churro's cab smelled like
beef jerky and had the worst rap music ever on
full blast. I wished he had HotLanta 95.7 on in

here. Mom said the station agreed to have PS on the morning show because their latest YouTube video (Heath pranking an unsuspecting Kyle and Zander by placing snakes in their bunk beds) had been picked up by late-night shows and now had almost a million hits. Turned out boys screaming like little girls was a real crowd-pleaser.

"Briggs said the air-conditioning broke in their tour bus and the boys are moody," Mom told me. "They better perk up before their first Lemon Ade show tonight."

I nodded like I understood, but it was hard to hear what Mom was saying over Churro's music. When we pulled up to the station, I noticed the PS tour bus with red flame decals in the parking lot, and my fingers started to tingle, which is exactly what Zander says happens to him when he's excited. I watched a tow truck pull up and start hooking chains to the tour bus. Mom paid Churro, and we bolted from the smelly cab as Briggs approached us.

"Piper, glad you made it," Briggs said, wiping his sweaty head with a paper towel. "What a night. I thought we would fry on that thing." He motioned to the tour bus and then turned back to Mom, all small talk over. "I told them they had a few press requirements this morning, but then they could take a few hours before sound check to catch up on sleep. They're exhausted, but they'll just have to chug some Roaring Dragon energy drinks and power on. This is an AM slot with Venus and the Flytraps, and they need to really kill it, you know?"

Mom pulled a leather binder out of her bag. "Not to worry. I've done some research on Venus's guest ratings, and I think I have some topics the boys can nail, sleepy or not. Is it possible to speak with them so that I can give the talking points to the DJs before their segment?"

Wow, Mom sounded so efficient and tour managementy. Even Briggs looked impressed.

"Sure, right this way," he said, leading us into the plain concrete building that looked more like a doctor's office compound than a cool radio station. "Mackenzie, we're happy to have you, too. My daughter, Jillian, is looking forward to having someone to hang out with besides the boys." Before I could respond, Briggs was way ahead of us, passing through security. Then we were whisked past the corporate offices and into the station area, where the boys were.

I could feel the shakes take over my body like I was doing the chicken dance at someone's bat mitzvah. Then my eyes started to water. My nose felt itchy. My eyesight started to blur, and I felt like I might throw up in the silver trash can we were passing.

I needed to calm down, but as we walked the long hallway, I had no idea how. Mac Attack would know what to do. She would blow into the greenroom with her nail file drawn and threaten anyone who made her feel uncomfortable. She'd banish them to the parking lot till her interview was over.

But me? I didn't have a nail file on me. The way I saw it, I had three choices: (1) I could ditch Mom and Briggs, find the nearest bathroom, and stick my head under a cold faucet to cool down (downside: I'd look like a drowned poodle when I saw Zander); (2) I could call Iris and Scarlet again and wig out (sadly, we had just passed a sign that said NO CELL PHONES); or (3) I could steal one of Briggs's Roaring Dragon energy drinks and "power on," as he'd told PS to do this morning.

Choice three made the most sense. On the Roaring Dragon commercial it says one sip makes you "feel the strength of the dragon coursing through your veins." Who cared if my cousin Rudy had a freak reaction to a Roaring Dragon last year? I couldn't see myself finding a trombone to run around playing for hours like he had.

"Come in and see the boys." Briggs nudged me through the door before I had a chance to react.

Suddenly I was standing in front of my favorite band, watching them snore. My stomach dropped like I was on one of those free-fall rides. Zander had an adorable puddle of drool dripping from his chin onto his Rolling Stones concert T-shirt, and Heath kept starting and stopping his snores like a leaf blower running out of gas.

Kyle was the only one sleeping dreamily, his blond head tucked into the couch pillows so that I could see only his left cheek.

"They should be up any second," Briggs said. "I told them they needed to have an energy drink twenty minutes before they went on the air. I ordered a case along with nongreen foods."

"Nongreen foods?" Mom repeated.

Briggs's cheeks colored slightly, and I jumped in, happy to concentrate on something other than the boys' being feet away. "Zander hates anything green."

Mom gave us a strange look before scribbling something in her leather binder. Then she went straight to a table in the corner to review her PS notes. Briggs followed her.

I looked around the room. The walls were covered with autographed pictures of musicians who had been to the station before and mementos like a guitar from Adam Levine. The funny thing about the greenroom was that it wasn't

71

green at all (which was a good thing, since Zander would have hated that). It was pale beige and really needed a touch-up. Over my head were speakers piping in Venus and the Flytraps' show. I heard the greenroom door open, and a ponytailed woman wearing a headset popped her head in and looked at me. "Perfect Storm is on in twenty minutes."

I felt very important being given this information, like I was really part of the band. "They'll be ready!" I said, and saluted. She looked at me strangely and ducked back out.

"Mac? Can you hand the boys their Roaring Dragons?" Mom asked. "They should drink them now so we have time to talk before they go on."

Wait. Mom wanted *me* to wake the boys up? Because I would if my hands weren't shaking. Maybe if I had my Roaring Dragon first, I could manage to do that. I tiptoed over to the table where a dozen Roaring Dragons were stacked in an artful display and took one off the top, making sure Mom wasn't watching. She does not approve of energy drinks for twelve-year-olds ("You have enough energy!"). I popped the can as quietly as I could. The Roaring Dragon smelled like cotton candy. I downed it as fast as I could, even though it made my head hurt. It tasted awful! Then I grabbed three more cans for the boys. Through the speakers I heard Venus start playing Lemon Ade's new single, and the beat was so catchy it made me want to dance.

Briggs clapped his hands, and Kyle started to stir. "Boys, time to rise and shine. You'll sleep when you're no longer musicians," he said with a chuckle, and I noticed he was bopping along to Lemon Ade, too. Headset Girl was back, and even she was smiling as she danced in place while Mom handed her some notes for the DJs. The greenroom was turning into one big party. I was sure the guys would wake up and be in a good mood, too.

Holding the boys' drinks, I danced my way

back to the couch where Zander was sprawled out, his legs in Heath's lap. I mentally rehearsed what I was going to say to him, unwrinkled my shirt so he could see it clearly, and then prepared to pop open the can. Zander deserved the first one. After all, he was the face of the band. I touched Zander's arm. (I TOUCHED ZANDER'S ARM!) "Zander? I have a Roaring Dragon for you." He began to stretch, and I noticed his right eye open before his left one (they were so blue!). He wiped the drool from his chin onto his jeans.

"Who are you?" he said, sounding still asleep.

OH . . . MY . . . GOD . . . he was talking to me! This was it! This was the moment I had been waiting for. I danced in place to keep down my nerves. Wow, that Roaring Dragon worked fast. I started to open the can. "I'm Mackenzie, we met at . . ."

"Mac, don't shake the . . . ," I heard Mom say, but it was too late.

The can in my hand popped open, and a hissing sound emerged, followed by a spray of green liquid flying in a million different directions. My big moment with the guys was being destroyed by a stream of green soda.

Wednesday, February 24
(I'm back to continue my story after a
quick bite for dinner!)

**LOCATION: Still Tour Stop #1—Atlanta, Georgia (or as it will forever be known: the Place Where Mac Caused the Roaring Dragon Nightmare)**

I watched in horror as the Roaring Dragon Nightmare unfolded in what felt like slow motion.

Zander stepped on Heath's stomach as he scrambled to jump over the back of the couch.

"Dude, watch it!" Heath barked, leaning back so that he wouldn't be hit by the offensive drink.

Heath stood up, slipped in the soda that had puddled on the floor, and went down hard. Briggs ran to help him up, but he slipped, too, and fell right next to Heath in the middle of the now-green floor.

*Green.* Green soda. Zander hates green soda!

"AAAH! GET IT AWAY!" Zander was pinned against the wall like the Roaring Dragon was acid. And all I could do was stand there helplessly and wait for the soda geyser to stop exploding like Old Faithful.

Someone pulled the can from my hands. I looked through the sticky soda haze and saw Kyle. He tossed the still-oozing can into the nearest trash can. "Are you okay?" he asked me as Mikey G. burst through the doors.

"What happened?" Mikey G. barked, sounding like he was seconds away from making us all drop and do twenty push-ups on the floor. I looked around the room in shock.

The scene wasn't pretty. Green soda dripped from the walls and covered the floor. My hair was sticky. Headset Girl was helping Briggs up and slipping. Heath was clutching his stomach in agony, and Zander was muttering to himself as he pulled off his wet concert tee. Mom gave me a look that could melt plastic.

"Look what you did!" Zander growled at me. His blue eyes were anything but tender like in their music videos, and I felt my lip quiver. "What am I supposed to wear on-air now?" He looked at Briggs, who began unbuttoning his wet Hawaiian shirt. "I'm not wearing *that*. Mikey G., can you run back to the bus and get me a new shirt?"

"No can do. The bus was rolled away to the shop," Mikey G. said apologetically. "We took your luggage off and brought it to the hotel already."

"Seriously?" Zander was flipping out. "I have to go on-air looking like this?"

"Well, it's not like anyone is going to *see* you," Kyle said in the cutest British accent.

"Kyle's right," Mom agreed. "This is a radio broadcast. We'll get you a change of clothes before the photo shoot for *Atlanta Monthly* that's scheduled for noon." Zander mumbled something under his breath, not realizing that my mom is the queen of deciphering mumbles. I saw her nostrils flare. "Forget the T-shirt, and let's concentrate on wowing the show hosts."

"You heard Piper," Briggs said in an upbeat voice. "I want you boys on your toes with Venus. Talk up Lemon Ade like she's the next queen of America. You know, if we had one." He slapped Zander on the back, and soda splashed off his shirt. Briggs winced.

Zander sighed. "Fine. I'll give them my Zander charm."

Heath snorted.

"Shut it, Heathcliff."

"Dude, I told you to stop calling me that!" Heath grumbled.

Zander turned to me and scowled. "Who let her in, anyway? I said no meet and greets with fans today."

I blinked back tears. "I'm really sorry about what happened," I sputtered, but Zander looked unmoved. "I was only trying to help."

"I guess Mac is technically a fan," Mom added. "But she's also my daughter."

Now it was Zander's turn to look foolish. "Sorry. We had a long night. It's nice to meet you," he added awkwardly. "I'm going to clean up before we go on the air."

Meet? But we'd met before. Didn't he recognize my shirt? He had said he loved it at Song Slam. "Have a good interview," I squeaked, but Zander was already gone. Mom gave me a sad smile as she followed Briggs out behind him.

"If it makes you feel better, I thought that was pretty funny," I heard someone say. I turned around. Heath was speaking to me. Kyle stood behind him, leaning against the wall, smirking. He was the only one who'd avoided the Roaring Dragon explosion altogether.

I quickly wiped my eyes with my shirt. I didn't want them to see me crying. I couldn't believe my first morning on the tour was going to be remembered as the Day of the Roaring Dragon Nightmare.

I heard the door to the greenroom fly open, and a girl my own age stood in the doorway. "Did I miss it?" she said, sounding out of breath. "Is it over? I heard Zander took a green-soda bath!"

Heath and Kyle started to laugh. "Dude was ready to be hosed down by a hazmat team!" Heath said. "You should have seen his face, Jilly." Now she started laughing, too, and I wanted to curl into a ball and rock back and forth. "You can thank Piper's daughter here for Zander's break-down. She shook the can of Roaring Dragon before opening it."

"Piper's daughter?" She looked at me and darted over. "You must be Mackenzie!" Her high voice sounded super friendly, and she had a smattering of freckles across her nose. She was taller than me by about two inches, and super lanky. We hadn't officially met that night I fainted backstage at Song Slam, but I had seen her there. "I'm Jillian, Briggs's daughter. I'm so glad you're here!"

I'd seen Jillian in a few of PS's videos. They liked to prank her, too. They called her Li'l Sis or Mini-Briggs. I had a feeling she knew the guys better than anyone. Maybe she could give me some Zander tips.

▷   ◁⟩) 00:25                                    100,000 views

JILLY GETS PRANKED!!

🖒 LIKE
Uploaded by Perfect Storm                          ∞ LIKES!!

Jillian shook my hand vigorously. "Thanks so much for deflating Zander's ego a bit. This day needed a pick-me-up after last night's heat hell on the tour bus. Zander needed a bath anyway. He stinks! Literally." Jillian rolled her eyes as she pulled her hair out of a bun piled high on her head. It fell to the middle of her back, hitting the top of her cute royal blue tank top. "No offense, guys," she said to Kyle and Heath, "I love you all like brothers, but man, can you clear out a tour bus."

"Um, we're standing right here, Jilly," Kyle said, his cheeks reddening like my own.

Jillian tugged at her Lemon Ade concert tank. She didn't seem to care. "The farting contests have got to go. When you can't open the bus windows, there is no way to get rid of that smell," she told me. "I'm soooo glad there is another girl on this tour," Jillian continued. "You have no idea how hard it is to hang out with roadies and these guys all day long."

"I'm sure it's torture," I said, hoping to fit in with Jilly. Really, I was thinking it sounded like a dream come true. I felt the Roaring Dragon dripping from my face and tried to wipe the liquid away. That's when Heath grabbed my arm, turning it over to look at my wrist. I'd forgotten I drew on my forearm on the plane. It was a pen drawing of Thor holding his hammer.

"Did you draw that?" Heath asked. "Guys, look at this!" Jillian and Kyle leaned over my arm. "That's killer! I always wanted a magic hammer like Thor's."

"It's not a magic hammer, it's Mjolnir," I said. Kyle chuckled.

Heath's chocolate-brown eyes widened. His lashes were so thick it looked like he had eyeliner on them, but now that I was standing that close, I could tell he wasn't actually wearing any! And wait! Where were his tattoos? I guess they had been sleeves, just like Iris suspected. I had to tell the girls ASAP!

I shrugged. "I know my comics." I felt Mac Attack course through my veins. Or maybe it was that Roaring Dragon. I was starting to feel nauseous again. I grabbed a banana from the untouched food on the table. It was covered in green syrup, but I took it anyway.

"She's got you beat at comic-book stuff, Heathcliff!" Jillian declared with a laugh.

"I wish everyone would stop calling me that," he whined.

Jillian stared at my outfit. "Hey, I know that shirt! The guys showed them to me in New York. Are you the girl who made them?"

I nodded.

"I sent that tee to my mum," Kyle said. "You're a good artist."

Wow, to his mom? "Thank you," I said shyly. Kyle and I stared at each other for a moment. Then Headset Girl popped her head in and waved for the boys to join her.

"We'll have to talk more about the Avengers soon," Heath said as he headed to the door. "Welcome to the tour, Mac."

Kyle gave a little wave good-bye.

"Thanks," I said, watching them go.

"Come on!" Jillian took my hand. "Let's follow them. We can make faces at them through the studio window while they're doing their interview."

By the time Mom and I checked into the hotel, I'd decided to add a Jillian character to the Mac Attack band. Her superpower? Laser-sharp memory. Jillian can recite street addresses for things like Zoo Atlanta and knows what time the boys eat breakfast most mornings (nine thirty).

Jillian might be the coolest girl I've ever met (other than Iris and Scarlet, of course). The two of us did not stop talking from the minute she said, "I don't trust people who don't eat ice cream." (ME TOO!) She also hates cheese on her pizza just like I do! ("Why would anyone want to melt cheese on bread?" she asked, and I totally agree.) And she thinks of PS like brothers, so there's no Zander crush competition. We're also both afraid of sharks after seeing *The Sharkinator Lives!* But Jillian can swim really fast, so she doesn't think she'll be eaten by one.

At the end of the day she told me to call her Jilly, and I told her to call me Mac. It was a true sign that we clicked as friends.

"Are you sure this is a good idea?" I asked Jilly. She was driving a golf cart through the backstage area of Orlando's Amway Center. I held on to my seat so tightly my knuckles were turning white as Jilly made a sharp turn down a long hallway and almost rammed into a row of boxes.

This is why twelve-year-olds don't drive!

"Daddy lets me drive the golf carts all the time," Jilly said, hitting the brakes before speeding off again. "It's the only way we'll make it to the PS set in time."

"I'd rather live than see the show," I mumbled as a roadie jumped out of the way of our cart.

"Stop worrying!" Jilly said. "Look! There's the entrance to the seats!" She made a sharp left, and I almost fell out of the cart. Jilly pulled to a stop near a set of massive double doors that led from the backstage to the concert seats. There was a big sign on them that said CONCERT IN PROGRESS. I heard a familiar melody coming from inside the arena.

"How you doing, Orlando? We're Perfect Storm!" Zander yelled. The crowd went wild, and I froze.

PS was about to open for Lemon Ade for the second time since I joined the tour, and for the second time I didn't want to go out there and watch the show for free.

I know, I know, ISN'T THAT THE WHOLE REASON WHY I'M HERE?

But I couldn't face Zander. The guys were still teasing me about the Roaring Dragon Nightmare. My first time meeting the boys as an official member of the tour, and I made a huge mess of things! Jilly said Zander had probably forgotten about the green-soda bath by now, but I was avoiding him just in case. In Atlanta, I had claimed the energy drink made me too sick to go to the concert. Now we were in Orlando, and I had told Mom I caught a cold from the traveling. Jilly wasn't buying it.

"Come on, Mac. I got Daddy to give us VIP stage seats, and I almost never get VIP stage seats!" Jilly told me, pulling her long hair into another bun without a hair tie. I still don't know how she does that. "You do not want to pass these seats up. They usually go to, well, very important people."

When she dragged me inside, I blinked hard to adjust to the dark. I was used to concert arenas being bright when you walked in so you could find your seats, but since it had taken Jilly almost an hour to convince me to come, the show had already started. We had to use our phone flashlight apps to find our seats. The

93

stadium was two stories high and full of people already standing and clapping along. I watched the lights onstage flash blue, then green, and finally land on Zander's face.

As soon as Zander started to sing "I Feel Blue," all my fears melted away. I stopped in my tracks to watch him, and soon I was daydreaming again about us running along the beach together, Zander alongside me holding a mic. . . .

"Mac? HELLO, Mac!" Jilly waved a hand in front of my face, snapping me out of my daydream. "Come on. You can see better from our seats."

Suddenly I didn't have to be asked twice. Jilly pulled me along till we got to the VIP section—a slightly elevated platform in the middle of the floor with three rows of seats. A runway led from our seats to the main stage. Mom and Briggs were already there. Behind them I could see the boys' families. Since they are all under eighteen, a family member has to travel with them. "Having fun?" Mom asked over the roaring crowd. Normally, Mom would be working backstage, but she had told me that morning she'd be watching the set to see how it looked from an audience perspective.

"These seats are amazing," I whispered, not wanting to interrupt Zander's singing. Kyle was playing the guitar, and Heath was sitting on top of a giant, glittery cutout of the letters PS.

"Five, six, seven, eight!" Heath shouted at the top of his lungs. He jumped off the letters and ran around the stage in ripped jeans and a vintage concert tee that said AC/DC. Sparklers lit the stage as the boys began singing "I Need You (Like a Fish Needs Water)."

I started singing along right away, and Jilly begrudgingly joined me. Soon I was so caught up in the music, I almost didn't see Zander POINT TO ME. Our eyes locked and he grinned. Was he going to walk down the catwalk toward me?

The shakes started again! I had to think clearly and channel my alter ego. Mac Attack would act like she couldn't care less if Zander walked the catwalk to sing to her— she'd probably grab Zander's mic and start to sing to *him*. There was no way I was going to do that. Instead I lip-synched the words and smiled as Zander continued to look at me. A piece of hair fell in front of his blue eyes, but he didn't brush it away. He just kept staring at me until—OUCH! A heel crunched down hard on my sneaker.

"You're in my seat."

I looked away from Zander and saw an older girl standing right on top of me. She was made up like a *Teen Vogue* model. (My mom lets me wear lip gloss most of the time, and eyeliner only on special occasions.) She had big blond hair that was held in place with enough hair spray to evaporate a new section of the ozone, and while I was still barely filling out my training bra, she had, um, a lot going on upstairs.

"Excuse me?" I rubbed my toes through my sneaker.

The girl rolled her eyes, which looked almost yellow in the dim light. "I said, 'You're in my seat.' Can you tell this little girl to move?" she asked an older girl behind her. "We should have three front-row seats. I'm Lola Cummings." She leaned in closer so I could hear her as the screaming intensified. "As in Lyle Cummings's daughter. Get it?"

"Who is Lyle Cummings?" I asked.

97

"My dad created the Wave One radio app," she said smugly.

I blinked. "Never heard of it."

She sighed. "You know, that app where you can personalize your own music stations?"

"I don't use that app," I said, already annoyed that she'd called me a little girl. "These seats were given to me, so if you could just move so I could see Zander, that'd be great."

"Aww, she likes Zander," Lola said, and clutched her heart. "That's so cute. Isn't she cute?" she said to her friends. "Aren't you out past your bedtime?"

Now I was getting really ticked off. "I'm not a little kid. I'm twelve."

Lola and her friends snorted. Snorted! "That's adorable," the one with the airbrushed PS tee said, and Lola nodded like a bobblehead. *Uh-huh. Uh-huh. Uh-huh.*

Out of the corner of my eye I could see Zander begin to walk down the catwalk. He was coming my way! I needed to get Lola out of here before she ruined the moment.

"Amber, who is my travel aide, is twenty-one, and my friend Bridget and I are fifteen, which is way older than twelve," Lola said condescendingly. "Actually, fifteen is the same age as Zander." Lola adjusted her purse straps, and those expensive bangles I've been begging Mom for slid down her arm. "I know all there is to know about Perfect Storm."

If she wanted a PS fact-off, I'd give her one. Zander had just stopped on the catwalk and was singing to some girls with a huge sign. I had a few minutes. "Really? What's Zander's favorite meal?"

She rolled her eyes. "Easy. A burger with cheddar cheese and bacon, sweet potato fries, corn peeled off the cob, and a brownie sundae for dessert." Bridget and Lola high-fived. "I also know the name of his first dog, his favorite color, and his favorite bedtime story. Daddy knows I worship PS, so he lets Bridget and me fly to all their concerts with Amber. And this seat you're in? It's always mine."

Not tonight, it wasn't. "My mom is the band's new tour manager, and Briggs himself gave me these tickets," I bragged, but it was hard to sound braggy over the roar of the audience scream-ing at the top of their lungs. Zander was getting closer. "So maybe you should—"

"Mac?" Mom touched my shoulder. "You're going to have to move seats, sweetie," she said apologetically as Zander drew closer.

She couldn't hear me shout no over the screaming girls. Lola, Bridget, and their nanny, or whatever she was, looked at me smugly.

"Lola's father just called Briggs to let him know she'd be here tonight." Mom smiled at Lola. "Please have a seat, and let us know if we can get you anything."

"It's about time," Lola said, nudging me out of the way.

I wanted to yank her hair. Mom must have sensed this because she pulled me into the aisle with Jilly. "Mac, I'm sorry, but Lola's dad is a big deal to this tour. If he requests front-row VIP seats for his daughter, then we have to give them to her." She grimaced. "There aren't any extra seats up here tonight, so you guys will have to watch from the monitor backstage."

"That's not fair," Jilly complained. "Lola is a spoiled brat who flies around in a private jet and is awful to everyone. She gets tickets to almost all their shows."

Mom winced at the ear-piercing screams. "Wave One is Lemon Ade's biggest sponsor, which means it's also Perfect Storm's. If we treat Lola well, who knows where it could lead for PS? I'm sorry, girls," she said as the three of us continued to stand in the aisle. "I don't like it, either, but we have to play along."

Just then I heard the screaming intensify. Zander had reached the end of the catwalk and was STANDING IN FRONT OF MY OLD SEAT. I watched as Lola and Bridget started to jump up and down. THEN ZANDER TOOK LOLA'S HAND AND LED HER BACK TO THE STAGE. Bridget practically fell to the floor convulsing.

"Typical," Jilly mumbled to herself as I watched in horror.

"What do you think, Orlando? Should I save this gorgeous girl from herself?" Zander asked the adoring crowd. "I think I'm going to sit her right here onstage for our whole set. Lola Cummings can be my lucky charm tonight."

I was supposed to be Zander's lucky charm tonight! He wanted to save me from me when he was walking down the catwalk! Now he was singing to Lola Cummings.

Jilly put her arm around me and led me away from the horror unfolding in front of us. "Don't worry, she doesn't come to *every* show.

Maybe you'll be the one Zander sings to in Nashville."

"Maybe," I said, but I felt like a deflated balloon. All I could think about was this old movie musical my mom likes called *Damn Yankees*. In it there's this devilish character named Lola, and lyrics from her theme song were now stuck in my head on repeat: "*Whatever Lola wants, Lola gets.*"

I just hoped this time the song was wrong.

## Sunday, February 28

As our tour bus cruised along the highway to our next destination, Mom and Briggs sat at the kitchen table going over Perfect Storm's schedule, Jilly watched a movie on her tablet in the bunk bed below me, and I recounted the Lola fiasco to Scarlet and Iris on the phone. They were very sympathetic. Iris promised to delete the Wave One app from her phone, and Scarlet declared Lola as her sworn enemy even though she had never met her. Despite their attempts to cheer me, I was still worked up over a tweet Zander posted after Friday night's concert:

**Zander Welling @zanderswell**
Orlando—our best show yet! And 2 the girl who
came onstage and all the others at the show—
every single one of you is cute as a button!

Zander didn't tweet anything like that after
he met me. Then again, Lola probably never
sprayed green soda at him.

The bus ground to a halt, and I heard the *click-clack* of Mom's heels. She had probably heard
me on the phone with Scarlet and Iris and was
going to give me a lecture about my cell phone
minutes. Instead she pulled the bunk bed curtain back and smiled. "Time for school!"

"School? Now?" I asked, staring at the dusty
field outside my window. Below me I heard Jilly
turn off the movie she was watching.

Mom nodded. "Yes. Get your shoes on. You're
switching to the boys' bus for class, and the
boys' families are moving over here, so you can
all concentrate on your work. You too, Jilly."

"No worries, Piper. I know the drill," I heard her say.

"Wait, you weren't kidding about me going to school with Perfect Storm?" I felt shaky all of a sudden, like I did after that Roaring Dragon.

"No," Mom said, glancing at the number on her phone and frowning. "Your tutor's name is Krissy." She motioned to a bag by her feet. In it were some of the school binders and notebooks I'd happily left in New York. Scratch that: thought I had left behind. "She already has your course work, and she's assured me she'll work with you privately to make sure you don't fall behind in your classes back home."

Great. "Work with you privately" sounded like code for "mucho amounts of homework."

Mom coaxed me out of bed. Jilly was already waiting by the door with textbooks of her own. "Let's go! We need to get you two on that bus and stay on schedule to get to Nashville on time."

I looked in a mirror as I walked to the front of the bus. I tried to pat down my bedhead and unwrinkle my wrinkled Captain America tee. I accepted the orange juice and bagels Mom threw at us as she shoved us out the door. The boys' bus was just ahead of ours, and I could see a petite, dark-haired woman waving us forward as we approached.

"Hello, Mackenzie Lowell!" she said in a voice that sounded like a cartoon mouse. With her gray pantsuit, she looked like a mouse, too. "I'm Krissy Pollicino, your new on-the-road teacher." She thrust three familiar textbooks into my arms as I went to shake her hand. "Time's a-wasting, so let's get on this bus and start a-learning!"

Jilly gave me a look and hurried on the bus ahead of me. Mom stopped to talk to Krissy about my "work ethic," as she called it, and I went on board. Perfect Storm's bus was nicer than ours. The couches were leather and didn't look bolted to the ground (even if they were). The large flat-screen TV was connected to every type of video game setup possible. There was a built-in bookshelf stocked with the latest DVDs, and guitars and sound equipment stored in compartments in the walls. The kitchen was tiny but still fancier than ours. Kyle was at the fridge, and I could see it was stocked with red Gatorade (Zander's fave!), chilled Oreos (more Zander!), and lots of strawberries (Zander again!). The cabinet Zander was currently opening had boxes upon boxes of Froot Loops and Cheerios inside. As soon as Zander saw me, he closed the cabinet and walked over. I started to panic. Was he going to yell at me?

"Hungry?" Zander asked with a smile. "We have tons of cereal if you want me to pour you a bowl before school starts."

Zander was going to make ME breakfast? Maybe he really had forgotten about the Roaring Dragon Nightmare!

"You're welcome to my private stash of Froot Loops, but be warned, I've, um, picked out all the Froot Loops that are the color—"

"Green, I know," I couldn't help but interrupt. Zander looked at me curiously. "I'm . . . sort of . . . a big fan." And now I was blushing.

"Really?" Was it my imagination, or did Zander just move closer? "What else do you know about me? I mean us—the band?" Jilly cleared her throat. I ignored her.

The words came flying out of my mouth before I could stop them. "Well, your favorite number is five, like mine, and you hate escalators, so I've sort of stopped using them myself. You hate green food, and you started singing when you were sixteen months old and fell in love with the show *Monster Rock*. You were singing at weddings by the time you were eight and had an agent by the time you were eleven and then were discovered by Briggs. The rest is history."

Zander smiled. "Wow, I had no idea you were such a fan."

MELTING!

"Okay, everyone, let's get to work!" Krissy said, interrupting my first good Zander moment. The two of us walked over to the table where Jilly, Kyle, and Heath were waiting. Heath seemed to be making spitballs. Zander took a seat next to him, and I slid into the only one left, next to Kyle. He gave me a little wave.

"Heathcliff, those aren't what I think they are, are they?" Krissy asked, her voice sounding way less mousy and sweet.

"No, Krissy!" Heath sang. "I'm working on that solar system project you gave me that is due this week." He smiled innocently and held up a small paper ball. "This is, um, Mars."

"Oh, good," Krissy said, relieved. "I don't want to walk off this bus with any notes or spitballs stuck to me again." Heath tried to suppress his laughter. "Now, if you'll all turn to your current social studies assignment and begin reading the next chapter, I'll help Mackenzie settle in." Zander yawned, and the others stared at Krissy blankly. "Textbooks! Now!" she said forcefully, and everyone began opening books. Krissy trained her big brown eyes at me. "Now, Mackenzie, your teacher tells me that you were studying the American Revolution, so I'd like you to start reading the chapter on the 1765 Stamp Act. You'll find that working with a teacher on the road requires much more independent learning, but the benefit is that you will become more self-reliant and that will help you . . ."

I tuned out and nodded as if I understood completely. What exactly did she mean by "self-reliant"? As in get my homework done on my own? Because I did that already. My mom didn't get home most days till almost seven. Did she mean "self-reliant" as in choose my own subjects to study? Because if she meant that, I was going to concentrate on art and get this first *Mac Attack* comic book done in no time!

"Since we're going to be on the road for most of the day, I've decided to work straight through our three-hour block and finish up before lunch," Krissy said, holding on to the kitchen counter as the bus started to move.

Everyone groaned.

"Three whole hours?" Heath whined. "Usually we work a half hour and take a break."

"I was in the middle of writing a song," Kyle spoke up. "If I wait three hours to finish it, I'm going to forget what I was writing about. Could I maybe get an hour break? Just this once?"

"No way!" Zander piped up. "Kyle isn't the only one who should get a free pass. I should, too! Piper and I are supposed to go over a list of radio stations we're trying to get to do interviews.

Remember how I wanted to mention you on your hometown station, Krissy?" I saw our teacher start to blush. "Well, how am I going to do that if I miss the meeting on radio stations? You *know* I'll make up the time later today. Please? I'm good for it." The other boys started talking over each other, and Jilly said something about life experience on the road trumping schoolwork.

Everyone was huffing and puffing and sighing and whining, and all I could think was:

*THERE ARE ONLY THREE HOURS OF SCHOOL A DAY?*

I was used to six plus! Three hours sounded like heaven, but I wasn't about to break from the pack and say this out loud.

"I don't want to hear another word about it," Krissy said tightly, "especially since no one came to see me in Orlando during my extra-help hours at the hotel." There were more sighs. "Now please start reading your assignments." The bus hit a bump, and I slid into Kyle.

"Sorry," I said sheepishly, and then I had a horrible thought. Did I brush my teeth this morning? Oh my God, I had been talking to Zander, and I probably had sleep mouth! I had to get some toothpaste STAT. The guys must have some. My arm shot up. "May I be excused to go to the bathroom?"

Everyone laughed. "This isn't a classroom." Zander gave me a big smile. "When you gotta go, go!"

"Bathroom breaks are the *only* acceptable breaks," Krissy agreed. "I need to make a call, but I'll be back to check on all of you soon." She headed to the front of the bus, and I went to the back. Our buses seemed to be set up the same, so I figured the bathroom would be just beyond the bunk beds.

Bunk beds that belonged to Perfect Storm! I didn't think it would hurt if I took a quick peek.

I pulled back the first curtain. I knew immediately it was Zander's bed. We both sleep on the

top bunk! That has to be a sign. Zander had a down comforter, fluffy pillows, pictures of himself with fellow celebrities, and a cutout of his face on a cereal box from Japan (the band is already huge there). There was also a big picture of him holding a Grammy, which the guys haven't won yet, and above it he'd written, "If you can believe it, you can achieve it." Zander is so dedicated.

The bunk below Zander's was super neat, and there were only a few pictures on the wall. It was Kyle's—there was a picture of him smiling with his family, a postcard of a London double-decker bus, a photo of a cute little white dog with a pirate patch covering its left eye, and

some lyrics pinned up to a corkboard. He really writes a lot!

When I heard Krissy reprimanding the group for a spitball attack, I knew I'd better hurry up. I quickly glanced at the third bunk and tried not to laugh when I saw how messy it was. The bed wasn't made, there were dirty socks and shirts piled in a corner along with Heath's fake tattoo sleeves, and Marvel superhero pictures were taped to the wall. As I closed the curtain, I noticed a Tigger stuffed animal peeking out from the messy sheets. I couldn't believe a guy like Heath slept with such a cute stuffed animal!

I had guessed right about the bathroom having toothpaste, so I brushed the best I could with my finger. But as I was leaving, I spotted a sign a little farther toward the back of the bus that said MUSICAL GENIUS IN PROGRESS. The guys' bus jam room! I'd seen it in their videos, and now I was *thisclose* to standing inside it. I looked up front again. I didn't think anyone would notice if I was gone just a *little* longer. After all, I was doing some *independent learning* about the band! I slipped inside and shut the door behind me.

"What are you doing in here?" Mikey G. asked as he jumped up from his seat on a tiny stool and fumbled with the remote to the flat-screen TV. As he moved around, notebooks fell off chairs, a guitar tipped over, and I caught a microphone stand about to tumble.

"I-I-I," I stuttered, staring at menacing Mikey G. He had to be about three hundred pounds of pure muscle. He was wearing a white tee that said DON'T MESS WITH TEXAS and jean shorts.

"This room is off limits!" I was afraid he was going to pop a blood vessel, he looked so upset. He kept pressing buttons, but the TV wouldn't shut off. I was about to apologize when I saw what he was watching.

"Hey, is that *Life After Life?*" I asked excitedly. "My mom and I love that show!" Mikey G.'s face went blank. "I'm obsessed with Crystal. She's so diabolical, you know? And Patrick Hamilton is so mean, I'm not sure if I want to hit him or take him to my middle school to scare all my teachers. Did you watch Friday's show? I could not believe it when—"

"That's just it!" Mikey G. interrupted. "That's the only episode that didn't tape, and you know the Friday show is always the cliff-hanger." I nodded sympathetically. "I can't wait till Monday for the recap." He started hitting remote buttons again. "The guys probably erased it as a practical joke, and when I figure out which one did it, he's dead."

I did not want Zander dying over a soap opera. "I could tell you what happened if you want." Mikey G. seemed interested, and when I say "interested," I mean he wasn't yelling, so I continued. "Let's just say someone's mother is no mother at all. She's Judith from the insane asylum, and she had surgery to change her face to Carla's!"

"No!" Mikey G.'s jaw dropped. "But Judith's car went over that cliff three weeks ago!"

"They never found the body," I said. "Marlee patched her up. She has a medical degree."

"Thanks for the recap." His eyes narrowed again. "Just don't tell anyone about this, okay? The boys know, but if it got out publicly, it could ruin my bodyguard cred."

Mikey G. could be scary when he wanted to be, but I had a feeling he was secretly a teddy bear. At least I hoped so. "Your secret is safe with me."

He smiled, revealing a gold tooth. "Good. Now get out of here!"

I hurried out the door again and made my way back toward the kitchen. Krissy was still on the phone, and everyone else was pretending to read but secretly doing something else.

"Did you get lost?" Heath asked, and they all looked up.

My hands felt clammy. They knew I was snooping! "Mikey G. was in the bathroom, so I had to wait," I lied.

"Geez, you're lucky—or not so lucky—the mate wasn't in there for an hour," Kyle told me. "He likes to read *Personal Detail Monthly* in there."

"Don't worry, Mac," Jilly assured me. "We don't usually have school for three hours in a row. Sometimes we have school an hour in the morning and then two hours later in the day."

"One time we had school at a McDonald's rest stop," Zander said, sounding amazed himself. "I wrote a personal essay on their fries: 'Deadly but Delicious.' Krissy gave me a B."

"So you can basically study whatever you want?" I asked excitedly.

"Well, no," Kyle spoke up. "At least I can't. I've got a different set of books than the others." He held up a history textbook with Big Ben on it. "But I think as long as you hit all your study requirements, you get credit. Krissy picks what we work on each day. She stays on top of our schooling and talks to our parents, or in my case, my older brother." I'd seen Kyle's brother around. Jilly had explained he was the only band member who didn't have his parents with him. Kyle's parents work at a university and couldn't get away.

"Krissy is on the tour full-time," Jilly explained. "It's the law that she be with us whether we're in school that day or not. She's got to work with us on independent study until we're sixteen and can take our GED or choose to keep studying on our own."

"See what I'm stuck with?" Heath slid over his textbook, which was open to a page on Pearl Harbor. "I asked if I could watch the movie and write a report, but she said no. How am I going to summarize a whole attack from a boring textbook?"

"My great-granddad was at the attack on Pearl Harbor," I told Heath, and all the guys looked at me in awe. "I did a paper on my great-granddad in January, and I think I got it back before we left. Maybe it's still in here." I looked through the folders Mom had brought from home. I saw the bright-red A staring from the pile and pulled the paper out triumphantly. "Here you go!"

Heath leaned over the table to high-five me before snatching the paper. "You're all right, Cap!" He pointed to the Captain America shield on my T-shirt and then to his own Hulk T-shirt, which said HULK SMASH.

Krissy cleared her throat, and everyone got quiet again. That's when I noticed the sticky note on top of the chapter I was supposed to read. "Write a report on the Stamp Act by this Wednesday!!!!!" it said with five exclamation marks. Gee, you'd think a teacher would use better grammar. Wednesday meant I had only four days. I groaned, and everyone looked up. "Krissy gave me four days to write my first paper, and it's on the Stamp Act from before the Revolutionary War."

"Maybe one of the big, bad Brits you Americans broke away from can help," Kyle joked.

"Oh, I . . . ," I started to mumble. Kyle was offering to help me? I glanced at Zander. He had tuned out of this conversation and was doing work again.

"My studies are pretty light this week," Kyle continued. "Don't tell Krissy I said that." He smiled at me, and I noticed how white his teeth were. "And I like writing. Papers are my favorite things to work on."

"'Papers are my favorite things to work on,'" Heath mimicked, and Zander threw a paper airplane at Kyle's head. They really acted like brothers.

"SHHHH!" Jilly hushed them, looking warily at Krissy.

"If you let me finish up this song I'm working on for a bit, we'll do 'independent study' and work on your paper together after," Kyle suggested.

"Okay," I said, pleasantly surprised. "That would be great. Thanks."

Kyle pulled out his notebook. I noticed there were song lyrics all over it. His book looked a lot like my journal—minus the artwork. I took out one of my notebooks that didn't have PS pictures drawn all over it. This one had a drawing of Cody, the dog next door.

"Brilliant!" Kyle pulled my notebook to him before I could stop him. "You drew that?"

125

"Mac is an incredible artist," Jilly said proudly.

Zander glanced at the book and smiled at me. "Ever draw a picture of the band or me?"

I started to giggle nervously. I mean, Zander was staring right at me!

Then Kyle hit Zander on the head with one of his notebooks. "Oi, mate! She drew us those T-shirts back in New York! Remember?"

"Oh yeah," Zander said, looking at me blankly. "Right . . . I think so."

Krissy cleared her throat again, but this time it sounded like a bullhorn. Some mouse she was turning out to be. All eyes went back on their books—except mine.

I looked around the table at everyone pretending to read as the countryside flew by. Jilly was whispering to Heath, and Zander kept stopping what he was doing to scribble on Kyle's book. In just a few minutes Heath had a fresh pile of spitballs ready. I smiled.

I had a feeling going to school on the road with these guys was going to be fun.

We survived our big three hours of school on Sunday, then the rest of the day took a major left turn. Hours before we were scheduled to be in Nashville, we got a call from the other bus. Briggs said the boys needed to do a last-minute radio interview with a Nashville station that was getting hundreds of requests a day for "I Feel Blue." They'd have to go straight from the radio station to the Grand Ole Opry that night to perform with Lemon Ade, but Mom said it was worth it. Wave One's app had calculated that thousands of people had already created Perfect Storm stations since Zander pulled Lola onstage in Orlando, and the boys' social media follower totals were continuing to climb.

Score: Lola 1, me 0.

It was a hectic Sunday night, but the good news was that Lola didn't make it to Nashville! And we're staying here till Thursday, which means I'll actually be able to sleep in the same bed for more than two nights in a row! We even had today off just to chill out and sightsee (after schoolwork, of course), and Mom promised we'd check out the life-size replica of the Parthenon at Centennial Park. Jilly told us there's an art museum inside it and a forty-two-foot statue of Athena with a six-foot replica of Nike in her right palm.

The bad news was that Jilly couldn't stay in Nashville to sightsee with us. She flew out for her stepbrother's birthday this morning and will meet up with us again in San Antonio, Texas. Thankfully, I have Mikey G. around to keep me company while Mom does tour manager stuff.

130

Mikey G. texted me (I have his cell number!) that he read Peaches and Raul are getting back together on *Life After Life* this week. We even made plans to watch it together!

For a few days I'm the only girl on the road with PS (well, if you don't count my mom). This is the perfect time for me to get Zander's attention. If I was ultracool like Mac Attack, I'd know what to do. Unfortunately, I'm anything but cool. As evidence may I present the Roaring Dragon Nightmare.

So when I saw a tweet that Zander posted this morning about how he couldn't sleep in Nashville and was up early, I jumped out of the comfy hotel bed, got dressed, and began pacing the hallway, hoping to bump into him. The hotel hall was quiet. To get to our floor, you have to have a special room key. That key also gives us access to a rooftop restaurant and room service menu. Zander and I are sleeping seven rooms apart—not that I'm counting—so it wasn't hard to keep an eye on his door. I was hoping I'd run into him and he'd say: "Mac, what are you doing today?" And I'd say, "Sightseeing. Want to come?" and then we'd see Nashville together and talk about our love of the Caribbean.

But by ten AM my hope for that happening was beginning to fade. Zander had a handwritten note taped to his door that said "Trying to get z's. Don't knock!"

I gave up hope and decided to just steal Zander's note and send it to Iris and Scarlet. My fingers were inches from the hotel stationery when I heard a whooshing sound. I looked down the hallway and saw twin boys running with cans of whipped cream in their hands. It was Heath's brothers, who had flown in with their mom for the week. I watched as they stopped every few feet to spray each other. It would hit their faces and the walls behind them, and they'd let out a deafening squeal. I pressed myself against the wall next to Zander's door to avoid getting hit. What were they doing? And where, as my mom would say, was their mother?

"Tristan and Isaac!" Heath yelled. He jumped out of a doorway in front of them in a white tank top and ripped jeans. He had dyed his hair blue. "What do you think you're doing?" The boys hung their heads. "You're supposed to shoot like this!" Heath pulled a can from his back pocket and shot them in the face. They immediately returned fire and ran down the hallway at lightning speed, laughing. I was about to get run over.

One of the twins stopped when he saw me cowering. A smile spread across Heath's face when he realized it was me. "Get her!" Heath shouted.

I took off running, but it was no use. The three of them were on me in seconds. I felt something cold and wet hit my thigh, and I immediately regretted wearing shorts this morning. The next shot took out my left ankle. The third hit my right elbow. I ran to the doorway between the hall and the elevator bank and tried to shut the fire doors for protection.

"Here!" Heath yelled to me, and I was surprised to see him toss me a can. "Defend yourself. You're outnumbered, so I'll join your team." We yanked one of the heavy metal doors as hard as we could to form a barricade.

I looked at the can. "Whipped cream? Really?"

Heath's blue hair was now covered in goo, and his tan face had white blobs dripping down his cheeks and chin. His brown eyes were mischievous. "Of course. I ordered an ice-cream sundae bar to my parents' room when they left to go jogging, Briggs is down at the gym, and Mikey G. is lifting weights. There was no one around to stop me," he said triumphantly, "which is why I thought giving the twins a sugar high would be a great way to start the day." He laughed and shot at one of the twins' shoes. The kid went down in the puddle and couldn't have cared less. He jumped right back up and, with

134

a terrifying scream, shot a long stream of whipped cream at us. Heath angled the door so that it ricocheted back at them.

"HA! HA!" Heath cheered.

I couldn't help but laugh. I was in the middle of a whipped-cream battle in a hotel room hallway in Nashville, and my partner in crime was Heath Holland.

It was TOTALLY AWESOME!

I ducked as another shot of whipped cream flew toward my head. The second twin appeared around our corner with a bottle of Hershey's syrup. Heath dived in front of me, taking the shot to his white tank top like a true hero. "Do you really think this is a good idea?" I asked, frowning at the syrup dripping down the wall next to me.

"Hey! Chocolate is against the rules," Heath yelled at his brothers. The other twin responded by spraying us with strawberry syrup. Heath looked at me and stopped shooting. "Room service is free on tour. Didn't you know? You should order it."

I wasn't sure room service was free for me, and I certainly didn't want to find out the hard way when Mom was sticking a $150 bill in my face.

"Shoot! Out of ammo." Heath dropped the empty can. "Time! We need to reload. Come on, Mac, I'll show you where I keep my whipped-cream stash." He winked at me. "I ordered a dozen cans."

Oh man. I did not want to see that bill.

I followed Heath down the hall as the twins

ran ahead of us. Heath was just starting to explain the art of aiming the whipped-cream can when we both heard a scream come from behind us. The housekeeping staff had just arrived on our floor. Looking around, I realized the carnage was much worse than I had thought. I winced. There was chocolate sauce on the doors, strawberry syrup dripping from the ceiling, and puddles of white cream everywhere the eye could see. One of the women started talking in rushed Spanish and ran to wipe down a wall. She fell flat on her face. I gasped. I ran toward the housekeeper to help, and that's when I heard a door slam behind me. The twins were gone. Heath shrugged as he began backing away himself.

"Sorry, Mac," he said with a crazy grin. "I'm already in hot water with Briggs for flooding the bathroom on the tour bus. I'm out, too."

Nooooo! "Heath?" I begged. "Don't do this to me. Heath?" He slid his key in the door, blew me a kiss, and was gone.

I was going to kill that boy.

If my mom didn't kill me first.

I tried to help the first woman up to win some brownie points. Another housekeeper started yelling, and my B-minus average in Spanish helped me make out the phrase "spoiled musicians" and "troublemakers." That's when several doors along the hallway started to open. Everyone wanted to see what the commotion was.

Zander popped his head out the door, which I happened to be standing in front of, and I caught a glimpse of his bedhead. When he saw the hallway, he burst out laughing. "Oh man. This has Heath written all over it!"

I wiped syrup from my brow. "What do I do?"

"Run," Zander instructed. "If Briggs or your mom sees this, you're—"

"MACKENZIE SABRINA LOWELL!" my mom yelled. "What happened here?"

Using my middle name is never a good sign.

"Good luck," Zander whispered, and warily started to shut his door.

My mom could seriously be a secret super-hero, because she was down the hall in seconds and caught Zander's door before it closed. "What is going on?" she asked the two of us as the housekeepers turned to her and started explaining in Spanish and major arm movements what they had found. Fortunately for them, but unfortunately for me, Mom understands the language much better than I do, and I watched the emotions flash across her face like a Vine clip. "No! You found them shooting whipped cream at each other?"

I gulped hard. I didn't know they had actually seen that part.

"We will clean up everything," Mom said, forgetting she was using English again. She ushered the housekeepers back toward the elevator bank. She spoke hurriedly in Spanish, and I noticed her produce some tickets from her pocket and hand them to the women, who seemed pretty excited. The women actually waved to me as they got in the elevator, leaving a bucket and some cleaning supplies behind. I waved back, and Mom gave me the *You're doomed* look. I quickly lowered my hand. As she stomped back down the hall, I heard Zander whistle. I shuffled closer to him for protection and winced when Mom's right heel caught in some syrup and she had to use the wall to steady herself.

"What were you thinking?" Mom's voice sounded shaky. "Defacing hotel property? Ordering room service and a DOZEN cans of whipped cream to start a battle in the hallway?" A drop of strawberry syrup fell from the ceiling and landed on Mom's hand. I thought I heard her growl. "Apparently, the whole staff is talking about the morning ice-cream sundae bar order, which is why housekeeping was sent up. You're lucky I was able to talk them down with concert tickets and promises that you two would clean this whole mess up."

"Whoa, Piper, the two of us?" Zander interjected. "I had nothing to do with this mess. You might want to check Heath's room, though. All the yelling woke me up, which is why I'm out here when I really should be catching z's. I was online with fans and radio stations till four this morning," he said, like this was supposed to impress my mother. It didn't.

"I'll go find Heath," Mom said, "but considering that the Super Soaker battle you three had backstage last night ruined a pricey speaker, I think you can pitch in here, too. Or do you guys want me to tell your parents what happened, since they were in the audience and missed the mayhem?"

141

Zander suddenly looked twitchy.

"Grab a bucket and start cleaning," Mom instructed us. "And don't think about leaving this hallway until the place is spotless." She stomped off to Heath's room.

I sighed and started walking toward the elevators to get a pair of rubber gloves and a multipurpose cleaner. Halfway there I realized Zander wasn't behind me. He was still standing in his doorway looking like a lost puppy.

"Mac, I feel like a jerk saying this, but the truth is, I can't touch cleaning products that aren't all natural." Zander looked pained. "Those chemicals are so bad for you. Think of what they could do to my vocal cords." He held his throat. "I can't risk losing my gift to clean up a mess I didn't make."

"Well, I didn't make this mess alone," I pointed out. "Your bandmate helped."

Zander's big blue eyes widened, and he leaned toward me, keeping one foot in his doorway. He held his hands in prayer. "Pleee-aase, Mac," he begged. "I'll make it up to you. We'll hang out later at the rooftop pool. Say four thirty? I'll make you one of my famous quesadillas."

Zander is always posting pictures of his quesadilla creations. It's his favorite thing to make with five nongreen ingredients. "It better be an amazing quesadilla if I have to clean up all of this syrup by myself," I said, trying to sound very alter-ego Mac.

Zander's face broke into a wide grin, and he offered me a high five. "You're amazing, Mac. See you later." He closed the door quietly behind him, leaving me to survey the damage.

It was going to take me hours to clean this up, and I had no idea how I was going to get rid of that syrupy smell. It reminded me of the Hershey's chocolate factory, but I didn't think the Nashville Hilton wanted to have that be its signature scent. I looked down the hall to see if

Mom had found Heath or the twins to help me, but there was no sign of them.

With a sigh I walked down the hall to retrieve the soapy bucket of water and basket of cleaning supplies. The elevator doors opened, and my housekeeping friends were back. The women placed a case of paper towels and a box of black garbage bags at my feet, then nodded and disappeared in the elevator again. I was starting to feel like Cinderella. There was no way I was making it to the quesadilla pool party on time.

"Wow, you botched this morning up good."

I looked up from the bottle I was opening to find Kyle in a black Ed Sheeran concert tee and khaki shorts. His blond hair was styled high above his head like it had been stuck in a socket, and his brown eyes were playful as they surveyed the scene around me. "Did Heath make this mess?"

"Yeah, but I helped," I admitted, adding, "Whipped-cream fight. It seemed fun till Heath and those mop-topped twin brothers of his disappeared and left me with the mess."

"That mate gets away with murder," Kyle said. He crouched down and started looking at my cleaning product choices. "Bugger. You could be here all day. Want some help?"

I stopped spraying cleaner on a paper towel and stared at him. "You'd help me clean up a mess you didn't make?"

He grabbed the sponge in the bucket and gave it a squeeze. Soapy water trickled through his fingers. "You did draw that awesome picture of Parliament for my 'My Country, My Home' project. Technically, I owe you. And besides— the quicker we're done, the quicker we can see Nashville. Jilly told me she gave you the skinny on the town, and I was hoping to see that big Athena statue hidden in some building somewhere and then check out some shops with Mikey G. You game?"

I didn't know what to say. Was Kyle really

inviting me to hang out with him AND helping me clean? Mom and I were supposed to check out the Parthenon together, but I had a feeling we weren't on the best terms at the moment. I could go again with her once she wasn't calling me "MACKENZIE SABRINA LOWELL" anymore. And since Mikey G. was chaperoning, I knew she wouldn't have a problem with me exploring the city. Still, I would have to ask her first. I wasn't about to have two strikes against me in one morning.

"I have to ask my mom," I said, knowing how young that probably sounded. Kyle is two years older than me. But he didn't blink an eye. I smiled and pushed the soap bucket closer to him. "But if she says yes, you have a deal."

He grinned. "Aces."

## Tuesday, March 1
*(I think. I'm not sure because it's so late at night and I'm writing this under the covers by flashlight so Mom doesn't get even more mad at me. Let me explain. . . .)*

**LOCATION: Sleepless in Nashville, Tennessee**

I have a confession: Everything I thought I knew about Kyle Beyer is WRONG!

Kyle is not quiet and boring. Kyle is ACES! (To quote his favorite word.) There's so much Scarlet, Iris, and the world don't know about him. Like: He started playing the guitar when he was only three! Then he taught himself to play the drums when he was seven! I never knew he was a songwriter, either. He wants to write songs for other artists and perform his own for PS. He wants to be the next Ed Sheeran (his idol). We talked so much about his songwriting and my artwork today that I nearly lost my voice!

Kyle's from England, and he told me this was his first time seeing most of America, so he was trying to soak it all in. I told him that I hadn't seen much of the States, either, but that I'd let him pick the sightseeing stops in Nashville. Mikey G., Kyle, and I took pictures in front of the Bluebird Cafe, which is this famous restaurant where you can go and listen to live music. Kyle

was gaga over it because all these big country stars play there, so I didn't tell him I only knew the place from watching *Nashville* with my mom. We also went to the Nashville Zoo, where the

elephants were so close you could almost touch them. Then we were off to Centennial Park to see the Parthenon.

I've never been to Greece, but if this is what the real Parthenon looks like, it's incredible. And huge! So is Athena! We walked around for a bit, and Kyle and I took pictures of ourselves in front of the Parthenon doing goofy poses. We made Mikey G. stand on the hill and look like he was holding up the Parthenon, which was pretty funny. Kyle put the shot up online and tagged me. Of course Scarlet and Iris texted me immediately.

SCARLET'S CELL: Saw post. ARE YOU OUT
W/ KYLE?

IRIS'S CELL: Kyle just tagged U on Instagram!!
Where is Zander? What's up???

I feel a little guilty saying this, but I didn't
see their texts till much later. I had my phone on
vibrate. I didn't want my phone ringing while we
were chatting over ribs at Jack's Bar-B-Que, which
our driver said has the best food in town. Kyle
liked it so much that he bought himself, Mikey
G., and me key chains to take home as souvenirs.
(Is that sweet or what?) Then, after we all used a
dozen hand wipes to get the bone-licking-good
barbecue sauce off our fingers, Kyle started asking me about my artwork.

"My mum loved that T-shirt you designed
for us in New York. My dad said he wants one,"
Kyle said, and I tuned out for a moment because
the sound of his British accent was so soothing I

could have fallen asleep. "I bet all your drawings are aces."

Was it getting hot in this restaurant? I couldn't believe Kyle liked my work. "Drawing comics is my favorite thing to work on, but album art is a close second," I said. "I know album covers are practically extinct, but I like when a band puts up record art on iTunes." Kyle picked at a steak fry, his eyes never leaving my face. I couldn't believe I had his full attention. "I feel like the cover of an album should speak for the songs on it."

"Lady Gaga still uses album art," Kyle told me. "Have you seen the cover for *Artpop?* Jeff Koons, this brilliant artist, designed the sculpture of Gaga for the album."

If Gaga was still doing album art, then maybe designing covers wasn't lame after all.

"Have you ever thought about a cover for our band?" Kyle asked.

Now my face felt like it was on fire! I wasn't answering that question. "Um . . ."

Kyle wasn't clueless. "Come on! We're mates now, aren't we? You have designed something, haven't you?" Mikey G. looked from me to Kyle curiously.

Still. Wouldn't. Budge.

"I'll tell you what," Kyle pressed, waving a steak fry in my face. "I'll write a song about you if you show me your PS album art. You know you have some." He sang the last part in this beautiful voice, and a table of senior citizens on a day tour turned around and applauded.

Of course I had some! But what if Kyle hated it? He'd never show Zander the art if he didn't like it himself. I felt for my journal, which I always carry on me for safekeeping. It was tucked in my cross-body bag. "You go first," I blurted out.

Kyle laughed. "I can't write a song on the fly." He thought for a moment. "You've got to give me a week to write something good." I looked at him skeptically. "I promise I'll hold up my end of the deal." He flipped over a Jack's Bar-B-Que paper place mat, and Mikey G. handed him a Sharpie. Kyle wrote in big block letters: "IOU For Mac Lowell: Entitled to one free song about her. —Kyle Beyer"

Kyle handed me the place mat and I stared at it. Iris and Scarlet were going to go bonkers. Kyle was going to write a song about me! I smiled shyly. "Okay, we have a deal." We shook on it.

I felt for my journal again. Could I do this? Show someone other than Scarlet, Iris, and Jilly my fiercely protected, completely personal album cover art? Jilly had told me Kyle was super nice. I looked at him again. Having spent so much time with him that afternoon made me realize she was right. He had bought a kid a cone at Centennial Park, had made the senior citizens swoon when he carried their food, and when a PS fan spotted him, he had taken a bunch of selfies with her. Kyle wouldn't make fun of my drawings. I was sure of it.

I slipped the journal out of my bag and turned to the page I looked at so often. Then I gently slid it across the table. Kyle and Mikey G. leaned over the drawing and didn't say anything for a moment.

"That"—Mikey G. pointed at my drawing without actually touching it with sticky fingers—"is wicked cool." Did I mention Mikey G. hails from Boston? And being a bodyguard runs in his family—his dad was a boy band bodyguard back in the day for this group called New Kids on the Block.

"Mac," Kyle said quietly, locking eyes with me, "that is the *perfect* cover for our album. You have to show this to Briggs."

WHAT?

Those were the words I had daydreamed Zander would say to me someday, and now Kyle was saying them to me for real! I could feel every part of my body stiffen. "You think it's that good?"

"Not 'that good,'" he joked, making fun of what he called my American slang. "It's aces. The boat, the storm, the clouds—you've captured Perfect Storm in one small picture." Mikey G. drank his Coke and mumbled his agreement. "This IS our cover."

I was seriously going to slide under the table. "Stop," I said, blushing harder.

"Show Briggs," Kyle insisted. He shut the journal and pulled it to his chest. "Better yet, let me hold on to this and I'll show it to him."

"NO!" I shouted a bit forcefully, scaring a woman at the senior-citizen table who knocked over her soda. I gently took back the journal and put it safely in my bag. "I mean, I don't think today is the best day to do it, considering I spent the morning making a mess of hotel property."

Kyle laughed. "I think you're learning how to be a true rocker. You know what else is very rock-star-like to do? Use the rooftop pool. Want to head back and swim?"

OMG, Zander! I had completely lost track of time. "I'm actually supposed to meet someone there right about now," I said. I was probably already late. I pictured Zander pacing the pool looking for me, a soggy quesadilla in his hand. We needed to get back there STAT. "Let's go!"

It took us almost a half hour to get back to the hotel. I could hear my phone vibrating in my pocket. Did Zander have my number? *WHERE ARE YOU, MY LUCKY CHARM?* I imagined his text saying. What if Zander left the pool, and all I found was the Mexican food he left behind? And how was I going to tell Kyle he couldn't come to the pool? Zander had talked about the two of us hanging out. Could I just show up with his bandmate, too? A rash was starting to break out on my chest, which used to happen only when I thought of sharks and *The Sharkinator Lives.*

Then we walked out the hotel doors onto the rooftop, and all my worries changed.

"What the . . . ?" Mikey G. started to say.

"You guys made it!" Zander shouted. His hair was a nice mess of curls, and he was wearing an orange bathing suit and a blue tee that matched his eyes. "Kyle, dude, I texted you an HOUR ago!"

Wait, Zander had texted Kyle about quesadillas, too? It occurred to me as I saw the crowd that maybe Zander hadn't planned on us hanging out alone after all. My heart sank.

There were at least fifty people crammed onto the rooftop deck filled with couches, twinkling lights, and pool floats. They were dancing on tables, hovering near the edge of the pool, and swimming in their clothes. Heath was playing pool volleyball with a bunch of people I didn't recognize. The smell of fried cheese and tacos wafted over to the doorway, where Mikey G., Kyle, and I were standing, and I noticed a delivery boy from Ain't-Cha-Lada Mexican handing out quesadillas to girls in bikinis.

"Kyle, come on! Mackenzie, you too!" Zander called.

I started to giggle, and Mikey G. raised his eyebrows. Zander did want me here! "Okay," I yelled back, and started to stroke a strand of my hair absentmindedly.

"I don't know if this party is a good idea." Kyle frowned as the volleyball from Heath's game sailed our way and Mikey G. volleyed it back. "I thought it was just the guys and us tonight. Your mom is going to go bonkers when she sees this crowd."

But Zander had made me quesadillas. Okay, he had *ordered* quesadillas for fifty people, including me, but still. He had called me over. I couldn't leave now. Not when Zander had gone

to all this trouble. "We could stay for a little bit,"
I suggested, looking at Zander again but trying
not to stare. He was cute even with girls hanging
on him. Sure, it wasn't just the two of us hanging out as he'd promised, but we would still be
hanging out. That had to mean something.

"Mac, I don't think . . . ," Kyle started to say,
but it was too late. Zander was a powerful mag-
net. I felt myself being pulled toward the fan
club gathered around him.

"I loved your tweet last week asking fans to
put a picture of a hyena on Heath's head and

post pictures," said a girl who sounded a lot like a hyena herself.

"I almost died when you guys posted that YouTube video pranking Lemon Ade on her tour bus," another girl chimed in. "Putting a rubber spider in her Cheerios was soooo funny!" She laughed giddily, and I rolled my eyes.

"That was my idea." Zander put his arms behind his head and got comfy in a lounge chair. "Heath wanted to jump out and scare her, but I knew she'd freak over that rubber spider. I come up with most of our pranks," he bragged. "Maybe you girls could help me come up with a new one for this week's post. We've doubled subscribers."

"That's because PS is the best band ever," a third girl said, knocking a taco out of someone's hands to move closer to Zander. "I've been listening to you guys all weekend, ever since I heard 'I Feel Blue' on my Wave One app. I listen to it OVER and OVER. I think I might be the biggest fan you guys have."

I snorted. Everyone turned to look at me, including Zander. "Sorry, I couldn't help it. You're their biggest fan after a WEEKEND? I've been listening to them for a YEAR."

Zander smirked, but his groupies collectively growled at me. "Mac," he said, and pulled me through the crowd toward his chair. I sat down on the edge of it. He put his arm around me, and I felt like my head was on fire. "Everyone, this is my good friend Mac. She's going to be hard to beat as the biggest PS fan."

"Oh yeah?" The self-proclaimed number one fan stuck her hands on her hips. "Prove it."

I wasn't scared of these Lola Cummings wannabes. I launched into my Zander fact sheet—how he only eats red M&M'S, the escalator story, the time his mom found him putting his favorite toy in the oven because he was worried it was cold. I was so busy reciting facts, I didn't hear my mom approach us. Neither did Zander.

"Zander, do you want to tell me why hotel

security is holding back a group of over a hundred teenage girls in the lobby?" Mom asked coolly. She didn't acknowledge me. I had a feeling that was a bad thing. "They've had to call in cops to control the crowd. Two girls fainted and had to be taken away by ambulance, and another is hyperventilating, all because someone sent a tweet saying there was a Mexican-food pool party with Perfect Storm at our hotel tonight."

"You said to keep up the strong media presence," Zander told her. "What better way to do that than invite fans to a party? At first it was just going to be Mac and me, but then I thought, wouldn't it be better if I could invite hundreds of fans to hang out? So I did." He looked pretty proud of himself, but Mom was not.

"Can you girls excuse us for a second?" she said to the small crowd around us, using the same voice she uses at Starbucks when she wants them to remake her coffee. The girls floated away, but not too far because each wanted the spot that

164

was mine, right next to Zander. I started to leave, too, but Zander stood and grabbed my hand.

"Stay, please," he said with a smile. AND HE DIDN'T LET GO OF MY HAND!

Mom definitely noticed, because her jaw became very set. "I know you want to help with our social media, Zander, and I appreciate all you've been doing since we talked about it, but you can't go booking a party with fans without talking to me." Her voice was rising. "It's dangerous—there is a maximum capacity up here. And it's a problem for the tour security—you released your hotel information to the world. And third, this is something that has to be approved by management. What were you thinking?"

I could feel Zander's grasp on me tighten. Was he scared of my mom?

"I'm sorry, Piper," he said. "I thought I was helping. Did you see how many tweets we got from this? And the pictures the girls are posting on Instagram? They love us!"

"That's not the point," Mom retorted. "The press is going to have a field day—'Band Throws Pool Party and Causes Commotion at Nashville Hotel.' It wasn't smart, Zander."

The color was draining from Zander's face. I couldn't stand him having to face my mom's wrath. He was clearly starting to get worked up. His right foot was tapping, which happens only when he gets really nervous. "It's my fault!" I blurted out, and Mom and Zander looked at me. "Zander invited me to have Mexican food with him, and I suggested he send the tweet to fans in the area. I thought it would be a good fan encounter," I said, using one of the terms Mom always does. "I didn't know it would get so big. Zander was against it from the start."

"*You* suggested a Mexican-themed pool party?" Mom said skeptically.

I tried not to blink. "Yep."

Mom was quiet for a moment. Then she pointed to Zander. "Shut this party down." Zander nodded, and Mom looked at me. "I'm really disappointed in you, Mac. We'll talk about this later."

I felt my stomach tighten as Mom walked

away. Zander put his arm around my shoulder again. "Thanks for covering for me. I do NOT need to get in any more trouble with Briggs, you know?"

Briggs. I had forgotten about him. Was he going to be mad at me? At my mom? But all my worries went out the window as quickly as they had come when Zander continued.

"Being a pop star is all I've ever wanted since I could walk and talk. It's the most important thing in the world." Zander ran a hand through his hair. "I'm lucky to have you on my side, Mackenzie Lowell." He handed me a foam box. "The quesadillas are a little soggy, but I promise to make you a batch next time we're on the bus for school. We'll tell Krissy they're part of our project on Spanish culture. Deal?"

"Deal," I said happily, and watched him walk away.

Our Caribbean honeymoon was definitely back on! I couldn't wait to tell Iris, Scarlet, Jilly, and even . . . wait, where was Kyle? I looked around the party, but I didn't see him anywhere. I hadn't even gotten a chance to thank him for my best day on the PS tour so far.

## Thursday, March 3

It's a good thing Krissy gave me a two-thousand-word personal essay to write, because there's not much else I can do. I'm grounded! On the road. No more sightseeing. No cell phone. No tablet. Mom took everything away. Instead I've been working on another scene in my *Mac Attack* comic book.

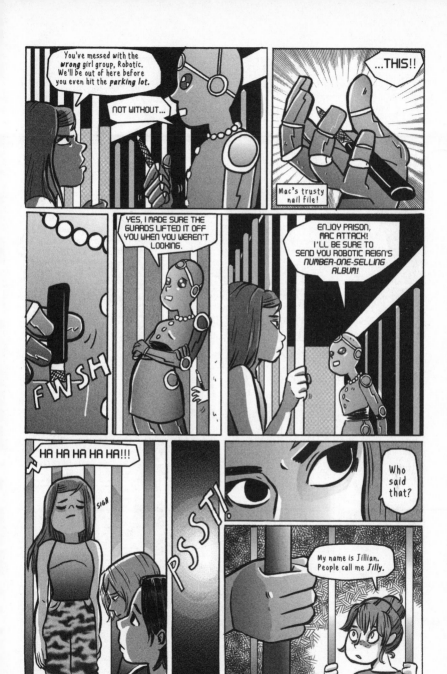

Being cooped up in a hotel room for days felt like jail. The room started to feel smaller than the tour bus, and the movies on demand were on a never-changing loop. Even more frustrating: Now that we are on the road again, I know Zander is only one bus away. We were finally hitting it off, and here I am, locked away in my tour-bus tower.

Why, God? WHY?

"You *know* why," Mom said when I whined to my monkey stuffed animal in the PS shirt (the one I bought at my first concert on the road with the guys). "Because you messed up." Mom stood at the edge of my bunk bed, but I wouldn't look at her. "Mac, I know being on the road with PS feels like the most incredible thing to ever happen to you, but I don't want you to lose sight of who you are."

I looked at her. "What's that supposed to mean?"

Mom's serious mood matched her style. She

had on a linen shirt and black trousers with open-toed heels, and her chestnut-colored hair was blown out in waves. She swears her hair dryer helps her do that, but it's never worked when I've tried it. I wondered if I'd ever grow up to look as put-together as she did.

Mom pushed the hair out of my eyes. "I like these boys, too, or I wouldn't have agreed to be their tour manager. Heath cracks me up, Kyle is a dedicated musician, and Zander is savvy when it comes to creating a public image. He really wants to know the ins and outs of the media world, which some artists couldn't care less about. But as smart as Zander is, he's still a teenage boy," she said sharply. "And teenage boys can be a huge mess, just like girls. Don't be so eager to hang out with PS that you're willing to forget who you are."

"I'm not," I argued.

Mom raised a well-arched eyebrow. "The daughter I know would never have thrown a food fight in a hotel hallway."

I looked down at my comforter. True.

"Not to mention you haven't set foot near a pool since you and the girls watched that ridiculous *Sharkinator* movie."

I pulled my comforter over my head and groaned. Also true.

"I had to do a lot of damage control for both the whipped-cream battle and the pool party."

More groaning on my part.

"Briggs and I had a long talk with the boys last night," Mom said. "They need to start acting like the professionals we know they can be. If they want the airplay and the fame, they need to start taking things more seriously. Otherwise, another band is waiting in the wings to take their place." Mom shrugged. "That's just the way this business works."

I shuddered. No Perfect Storm in the world? I thought of Kyle and his dreams of songwriting. Zander and his hopes to be the biggest band on the planet. Heath and his love of fun and adventure that always got the fans in the audience up and dancing. Could that all really disappear in a heartbeat? "Maybe the world needs to see the boys as we see them," I suggested.

Mom looked puzzled. "What do you mean?"

I thought for a moment about everything I had learned about PS so far that was different from what I had seen in their Instagram and YouTube videos. I sat up, suddenly excited. "Well, Heath can be trouble, but he's also a cool big brother. Kyle wants to be a songwriter and write original stuff for PS. And you said yourself how amazing Zander is with the industry stuff. He wants this bad. They all do."

Mom touched my chin. "You might have something here. I'm going to talk to Briggs."

I hugged my monkey (named Zander, of course) and started daydreaming about the band thanking me for all the positive publicity they'd gotten because of my suggestion. ("Thanks, Mac," Zander would say. "If it weren't for you, we'd be playing a state fair in Iowa. You really got us back on track. That's why I was hoping you would—")

"Mac?" Mom was calling my name. Oops! "I think you've learned your lesson. When we get to Texas, why don't the two of us get something to eat?"

I jumped up before she could change her

mind. "Okay! I'm in the mood for barbecue again. I went to this great place with Kyle in Nashville, and I keep dreaming of their ribs."

Mom laughed. "Barbecue it is."

By the time we got to Austin, Mom and I were back to being our old selves. We were a team again. I liked that.

## Friday, March 4

Friday morning Briggs knocked on our door at the evil hour of eight AM.

(Yeah, yeah, I used to be at school at eight, but road life is different!)

Mom opened the door and found Briggs in quite a state. His hair was wild, and it looked like he had football paint under his eyes. "You two have to come downstairs and hear this. We've been up half the night working on it, and it still doesn't sound right."

"Working on what?" I asked.

"A new Perfect Storm song," Briggs said.

My stomach did a back handspring (some-thing I can't do). I was going to get to hear a new song before everyone else?

"The bus is still parked in valet, where we left it when we checked in," Briggs added. "Get dressed and come have a listen."

Mom and I got dressed quickly (well, I was semiquick—I couldn't be seen with my hair this wild!). Then we headed downstairs and boarded the bus. I immediately screamed.

Jilly screamed back.

"What are you doing here?" I asked as the two of us grabbed each other and jumped up and down. Mikey G. was sitting at the kitchen table eating a bowl of cereal and reading *Soap Opera Digest*. He looked at us like we were deranged.

"I flew back a day early," Jilly said, her voice jumping with our jumps. "I missed you and the tour, and I can only take my pint-size stepbrother for so long."

I overheard Mom telling Briggs a little about my

idea, but then I forgot all about it because Jilly and I were busy catching up. She told me about her stepbrother almost setting the house on fire with his birthday candles, and I told her about the whipped-cream battle in the hallway, Zander's pool party, my grounding, and my day out with Kyle.

"Kyle, huh?" Jilly had a strange look on her face. The bus suddenly felt very warm. I wondered if the air-conditioning was broken again.

"Girls? Want to come in the back and hear the boys' new song?" Briggs asked.

He didn't have to ask twice. I was at the back of the bus in seconds, with Jilly and Mom right behind me. When I heard the strum of a guitar and humming as we neared the door, my heart started to thump madly. The boys were in a semicircle, and Heath and Kyle had guitars on their laps. Sheet music and scribbled lyrics sat on the floor in front of them. Mikey G., Mom, Jilly, Briggs, and I squeezed in around them. Zander was concentrating on the song lyrics, but

Kyle looked up and gave a little wave. I suddenly felt bad that I hadn't talked to him since our day out. I really needed to tell him about my stint in prison.

"Einstein sent us this song for the boys without being asked," Briggs said proudly.

That was impressive. Einstein is one of the biggest songwriters in music right now. He's written for everyone from Katy Perry to Carrie Underwood. If he had penned a song for PS, then

they were obviously starting to get noticed. I had heard Mom tell Briggs that their YouTube channel subscribers had doubled again!

"So what do you guys think so far?" Briggs asked the boys. "Is it album-worthy?"

Heath exhaled. "There's something about this chorus that isn't working for us. It's got no edge, you know? And there's only one lead on vocals."

"All our songs have one lead on vocals— me," Zander pointed out. He had his sunglasses on indoors, which is a pet peeve of mine. Sunglasses inside sort of defeats the purpose, but for Zander I was willing to make an exception.

"Why don't you try it for Piper and the girls, and they'll tell you what they think?" Briggs suggested before anyone could respond.

Kyle looked at the others, who nodded. Then he began to play his guitar, his fingers moving swiftly across the strings, making a melody that was fast and sounded more like a rock song than a pop hit. Seconds later Heath joined in. Zander was the only one without an instrument. I guess he doesn't need to play one when he has the voice of an angel. When Zander started to sing, I closed my eyes and listened without really trying to hear the words. It was always hard to catch them all on the first listen of a song, but I got the gist pretty quickly. They seemed to be about a boy who wanted a girl who wanted someone else, and the lyrics were . . . sort of dull. Zander sounded great, but Heath and Kyle barely did more than ooh and aah on the chorus. Usually a PS song makes my foot tap and my body bop along by the first chorus, but this time, nada.

Heath strummed the last note. "See?" He looked at us, and I looked around. No one seemed that impressed. Jilly was examining a chipped nail. Mom's jaw was set, and Briggs was wiping his sweaty brow. Mikey G. popped gum in his mouth.

188

Briggs looked at me. "Well? You're a huge PS fan. What do you think?"

Everyone looked at me. "It's—um—" There was no getting around the truth. "It's boring."

"See? The chorus is not catchy at all," Kyle said, sounding frustrated. "Our fans love a good chorus to sing along to."

"I like it," Zander announced.

"You would," Heath shot back. "It's practically a solo."

Uh-oh.

"I agree it doesn't have the right beat, but how do you ask Einstein to rework a song?" Briggs sighed. "I was hoping it would be so good we could record it right away and release it as a single in anticipation of the album. But . . ." He shook his head and looked at my mom. "Wave One wants us to find something that will be even bigger than 'I Feel Blue.' I don't think this is it."

So far PS had released only an EP, which is a smaller version of an album. They'd had a few singles but not enough airplay to be considered big stars yet. Wave One was responsible for getting them more radio time. Z100 had played their single only to promote them being in Song Slam, and now Mom was desperately trying to get the label's publicity department to get the boys on the morning show with Elvis Duran. She said one time on the show with him and the band would be unstoppable. I didn't know much about the music industry, but Briggs was probably right. The guys needed a hit.

Heath and Zander were still bickering. Kyle was scribbling more notes on the sheet music and strumming his guitar. He seemed lost in his own world—the world of a song meant for PS. That was it! "What about Kyle's music?" I blurted out, and Kyle stopped strumming. His cheeks colored slightly. "He's written a bunch of music for PS, haven't you, Kyle?"

"I didn't know you were writing music," Briggs said. "Why haven't you shown it to us?"

"Yeah." Heath poked him in the ribs with a guitar pick. "You said you were just messing around. You didn't say you had actually written something we could use. Let's hear it."

I gulped hard. I had put Kyle on the spot, and I didn't even know if he was ready to show his work yet. The two of us made eye contact, and I tried to send him a message telepathically like they always do on *Life After Life*: *You've got this.*

Kyle reached into the binder in front of him and pulled two sheets from the back. "Okay. This one is called 'Just Another Love Song.'" He passed pages to Heath and Zander, who looked surprised that Kyle actually had copies.

Maybe he was just waiting for the right moment to share this song, and I had made it happen.

Or maybe Kyle was never going to speak to me again.

Heath read the music over. I watched his

mouth moving. His head started to bop. "Can I get on the guitar, too?"

"Absolutely," Kyle said. "You okay with this, Briggs?"

Briggs threw his hands up. "Why not? Give it a go."

Kyle looked at the others. "Okay, ready and . . ."

As soon as Kyle started to play, I knew the song was special. It was a riff on love songs—making fun of how mushy some were and how they said things guys would never say in real life. Each of the guys had their own section to sing, and they all came in on the chorus, which had this great pop beat with a rocker edge. Heath was banging his head along with the music, and I could see Zander's toe tapping. Mine was, too. Forget Einstein! This song sounded like a PS song should. I looked at Jilly, and she gave me two thumbs-ups. The question was, would Briggs agree?

When the song ended, the room was silent.

We all looked at the decision maker. Briggs broke into a huge smile and started to applaud. "That's the song! It has 'hit' written all over it." He grabbed Kyle around the neck and pulled him in to give him a noogie, and we all cheered.

"Do you think the fact that Kyle's not a hit maker will be a problem?" Zander said, to my surprise. Zander wasn't going to ruin this for Kyle, was he? "The song is great—just great—but usually I do all the leads, and we'd share the lead on this number, so . . ."

"The song is perfect," Briggs said, and turned back to Kyle again. "Why have you been hiding this talent from me? We could have been doing stadium tours ages ago if you'd given us some material."

Kyle laughed, and I couldn't help but bounce on my toes. This was what he wanted—to write music he could perform—and now it was going to happen. I was so happy for him.

"I'm booking us studio time. Let's lay this down and make some tweaks before we lose this momentum. I have a feeling this song will send PS into the stratosphere!"

Everyone was clapping, but I couldn't help noticing that Zander seemed a bit down. Kyle was blushing madly. "Thanks," he mouthed to me.

I thought I might burst. "You're welcome," I mouthed back.

"We're going to leave you boys be so you can get back to work creating genius!" Briggs said, shooing the rest of us out. "One more hour, okay? Then you can sleep! Now go! Work!"

Briggs shut the door behind him and looked at my mom. He was sweating more than ever. "This is it. The hit we've been waiting for."

"Between this and the contest, I think these boys are going to have so much press they'll hardly be able to fit it all in," Mom agreed.

"What contest?" Jilly asked.

"Piper thought of it," Briggs told us. "I already looped in publicity. They loved the idea! They think this will give us a way to show the band's softer side."

Softer side? That was my idea! I beamed. Wow. Maybe I should consider a dual career—artist and publicist. I obviously have a knack for this sort of thing.

"We're offering fans the chance to win their perfect PS moment," he explained as his phone began to ring. "Fans write in to ask the band to do something personal with them—go on a date,

take them to the prom, join their soccer team—
and we'll narrow those wishes down to the most
innovative. The entry the boys like most will
win the fan her PS moment with the band."

"We're going to build on the momentum of
the Lemon Ade tour and rush entries in," Mom
added. "The PS fan club says it already has a
few thousand pieces of fan mail to sort through
from the last month alone. So between those
letters and the new entries we get in the coming
weeks, we'll have a lot to choose from. Some fan
is going to be very lucky."

*Some fan.* My ears started to ring. I was a fan. A fan who had written just that kind of letter myself before I knew Mom was going to get a job with PS. What if I was with the guys when someone found my letter and read it out loud? Sure, I had put my middle name on the poster so that I had a secret identity, but if they laughed at my poem, I would still feel tinier than a flea.

And what would Kyle say about my poem? He was such a talented songwriter. What if he thought it was stupid?

What if, what if, what if.

Who was I kidding? I was being paranoid! According to Jilly, there was fan mail collecting dust at the PS fan club headquarters, and they'd had thousands of new letters this month alone. There was NO WAY my little poem and drawing would be found and make it into the top entries. Perfect Storm would never see it.

Right?

### LOCATION: Santa Fe, New Mexico

Fact: I had to check my phone to see what day it was before I wrote it in my journal!

Second fact: I wasn't sure what city we were in when I woke up this morning!

I've always read in *Popstar!* magazine about bands who claim that all cities look the same from a hotel room, but I didn't believe them. Now I do! I feel like a Ping-Pong ball. In the last few days we went from Austin to San Antonio, Texas; made a stop in Oklahoma City, Oklahoma, for PS to do a photo shoot that label publicity arranged for the contest; and then were on to Santa Fe, New Mexico.

I feel like the only time I've seen my mom the last few days was when she was snoring in the bed next to me. After the craziness that went down in Nashville, I've been trying to stay out of the way. Z100 mentioned PS and their YouTube videos on the morning show a few days ago, and ever since then the band has been getting followers and requests like crazy! Mom can barely finish her favorite caramel lattes, let alone sightsee, so Jilly and I have found something else to do with our time. We've been holed up with Mikey G. on the bus getting Jilly hooked on *Life After*

*Life*. ("So Carmen is secretly a royal and looking for a prince, and Oliver doesn't have a clue?" she cried.)

Taking a walk down *Life After Life* memory lane has been fun, but today Mikey G. brought us to the Hilton down the block from the Sheraton we're staying in (pop-star rule learned in Nashville: Never host an event at the hotel you're actually staying in). PS was doing a fan listening session there that was being taped for PS's YouTube channel AND was being considered for a segment on *Today* about the rise of new boy bands. Mom wanted the room as packed as possible, and since the event came together on such short notice, Jilly and I were called in to serve as warm bodies. We were not allowed to ask questions, though (boo!). I was settling into my seat in the third row, watching girls trickle in as they saw the tweets from the boys, when Zander approached.

"Hey." Weeks later Zander's smile still had a

way of making me feel like the inside of a molten chocolate cake.

"Hi," I said back. (Obviously, this was a very exciting conversation.)

"I still owe you some authentic quesadillas, don't I?" Zander asked, leaning on the back of one of the folding chairs in front of me.

"Um—OUCH!" I replied. Zander looked at me oddly. Jilly had pinched me! "I mean, yes!"

"If there's time, maybe we can go to Poco Loco. Word has it that it's the place to go for authentic Mexican food," Zander said. "I know, I'm not cooking, but I bet this is better. You up for another chip-eating contest?"

This was what I got for winning the chip-eating contest against Jilly and the roadies the other night in Austin. How was I supposed to know Zander was watching me shove tortilla chips in my mouth at record speed? The prize was exclusive use of one of the golf carts backstage, and I was not passing up my own golf cart. I am a much safer driver than Jilly!

At least Zander had noticed I liked tortilla chips.

I could feel the giggles starting and then that overheated feeling I get when Zander is nearby and looking cute (today his hair was extra messy, and he was wearing a red bull's-eye T-shirt that looked great on him).

Jilly pinched me again and I recovered. "Sure, sounds fun."

"Awesome. My mouth is watering thinking about that food already." He winked at me. Or maybe he winked at the girl squealing behind me. I wasn't sure.

"See you after the show!" I said as girls around us started to give me dirty looks. My mind was already far, far away. I was on a beach with Zander, eating blue corn tortilla chips and talking about the first time we really hung out together, which would be today. This would be the moment Zander and I really got to talk. I bet we had a lot in common, like Kyle and I did. So far all we'd really talked about was his role in the band, what it meant to be in a band, and how much he loved the band. Zander as a person, separate from PS, I just didn't know yet.

"OH NO," Jilly said. "Not *her* again." I turned around to see who had gotten Jilly worked up.

It was Lola Cummings. She stood in the doorway carrying a mega-expensive designer bag and wearing a dress that showed just how much older she was than most of us in the room.

"Noooo!" I groaned. She was walking right toward us. Jilly and I sat there in our beat-up T-shirts, which we hadn't bothered changing because we didn't know we were being filmed, and our summer shorts, which were better suited for an outing at an amusement park than an on-air concert, and tried not to look bothered. But I was bothered, especially when Lola, her babysitter, and her equally annoying friend Bridget walked past us and went right for the FRONT ROW. They sat down in three reserved seats just as the lights began to dim and Briggs was telling the audience about being taped and waivers and other things I didn't care about at that moment.

So instead of concentrating on the boys and listening to them talk about how they had become a band (I already knew the story) and how Lemon Ade had picked them to open on her tour, I was staring at Lola's big blond head, getting more annoyed every second. I could picture her smiling at Zander and giggling at his every word ("You mean, like you do?" Jilly asked). When the listening session was over, I made a beeline to the front row, where Lola was talking to Zander.

"There you are!" Lola cooed, linking her arm through mine.

Exsqueeze me? I unhooked my arm STAT!

"I was just telling Z. that they have the best clothing boutiques in town. Daddy told me to buy Zander some new threads for his next few shows." Lola's glossy pink lips were way too close to my face.

"Too bad he's already having lunch with Mac," Jilly said, and I realized she was standing behind me, legs spread, arms crossed, looking like a mini Mikey G.

"Are you doing a *sixth-grade* paper on Zander or something?" Lola started texting someone on her phone, then got bored and handed her phone to her babysitter to text for her.

"I'm in seventh grade," I told her, feeling small but hoping I didn't look it.

"So, Zander, how about it? Want to shop? We can alert the paparazzi so they can get some pics." She looked at me. "Being seen with the daughter of the Wave One owner is great press."

"Is it?" Jilly asked. A girl pushed her from

behind to get a selfie with Zander. "Because I don't think I've ever seen a picture of you in *Popstar!*"

Lola's eyes narrowed. "That's because they post my pictures online to reach fans faster."

Zander stopped scribbling autographs. "Sorry, Lola. I actually do have plans with Mac."

Score: Lola 1, me 1. HA!

"But I have to cancel." Zander flashed me those puppy-dog eyes.

What?

"Publicity scored me some meetings with radio executives in town, and they're going to take me to lunch to talk about PS stuff we can do together. You don't mind, do you?"

"Of course not," I said, and tried not to sound disappointed.

Zander looked relieved. "Thanks, Mac. You know how important this is."

I did. I watched him turn around to sign more autographs. I tried not to look too dejected. Lola stomped off in a huff herself, and a local reporter began interviewing Zander.

"So, is there a special girl in your life?" the reporter asked.

"Girl?" Zander played to the camera. "Every girl is my girl—I'm doing my job for them. I love making girls happy." More screams.

"I mean a girlfriend," the reporter pressed. "Do you have one?"

Zander laughed. "No way! I don't have time for a girlfriend." A few girls nearby gasped. "But I'm always looking for that special someone to make me change my mind."

I felt like a bouncy house that had just sprung a leak. Zander didn't want a girl in his life right now. And if he was looking for that special someone to change his mind, that special someone obviously wasn't me.

"You okay?" Jilly pulled me out of the conference room and into the lobby, where Mikey G. and the extra security were ushering girls out of the hotel. Briggs was going over something with the videographers he'd hired, and Mom was on the phone again. "You'll come up with something way better to do this afternoon," Jilly assured me. "I just wish I could do it with you. My mom flew in on her way to Lake Tahoe, and we're going to the spa." She made a face. "Like I want to spend hours getting a manicure!"

With all of Jilly's basketball playing with the roadies, a manicure was going to chip in an hour. "I'm sure you'll still have fun hanging out with your mom," I said, trying to be optimistic. "Mine

is so busy this week, I don't think she remembers what I look like."

"Of course I remember what you look like."
Mom put an arm around Jilly and gave her a hug.
"Hmm . . . you do seem a tad taller, though, and
I don't remember you biting your nails, either."

"Mom!" I swatted at her. "That's not funny!"

My mom hugged me and held on extra long.
"What are you up to today? Any chance you
want to check out Santa Fe with your mom? Jilly
texted me a list of places to see while we're in
town, and I know one you'd love—Comic Book
University."

"They have the largest archive of comic books in
America," Jilly said. "There are comic-book classes
you can take, a museum of original comic-book
art, and a library where you can read everything
from *Ant-Man* to *Fantastic Four* to *Fables*."

"I love *Fables*," I said, shocked that Jilly knew
the name of a comic-book series about fairy-tale
characters who secretly live in New York.

"Then let's go read some," Mom suggested, and shockingly, she put her phone on VIBRATE! She *never* does that. "I told Briggs I'm off duty for a few hours."

"Can you do that?" I was nervous. The last thing I wanted was for Mom to lose her job.

"Yes," Mom said with a laugh. "Briggs is going with Zander to his lunch meetings, and the video has to be edited before they can send it over to *Today* and Z100 for consideration, but if they like it . . ." Mom exhaled slowly. "Publicity says Elvis Duran might invite the boys on the morning show to play their new single."

Things were definitely changing for PS now. If Z100 came calling, they could go from a cute opening act to a band that not just Scarlet, Iris, and I loved, but that the whole country swooned over.

It was almost too dizzying to think about.

"Ready?" Mom hiked her purse on her arm and slipped her phone inside.

"I think so," I said, leaving the screaming girls, Perfect Storm, and the hotel behind for a normal afternoon with my mom. Which wasn't so normal, when I thought about it. Our new normal involved quick conversations over a bagel for me and a protein bar for her, or the usual "Brush your teeth before bed, Mac" request I got every night at lights-out. I'd fall asleep to the glow of her computer screen as a night-light and Mom still typing away on it in the background.

"Before we go in, I want to apologize to you," Mom said as we stepped out of the cab in front of Comic Book University. Her brown eyes looked sad. "I thought this trip would be a chance for us to spend more time together, but I feel like I've been busier than ever."

I stopped short in front of the pink building with the slate roof. "Mom, are you kidding? This has been the best trip EVER!" I grabbed her hand and held it, which was something I knew I didn't do much now that I was older. "I love seeing all these cities, hanging out with Jilly, and seeing what it's like to be on the road with a soon-to-be-megafamous boy band."

Mom's face relaxed. "Good. Sometimes I feel like a rubber band stretched too thin, but as long as you're having a good time, I'm happy."

"I am happy, and you know why?" I never answered my own question. I felt the cool rush of the air-conditioning and saw all those comic books waiting for me and forgot everything else. This place had comic-book wallpaper, lithographs, and priceless action figures in glass cases. There was a huge red banner hung across the back wall that said COMIC BOOK UNIVERSITY. Behind it was another room with computers, racks of comic books, and a sign that said COMICS CLASSES IN CLASSROOM #3. I screamed without meaning to.

213

Mom frowned. "It's smaller than it looked online."

Who cares if it was tiny? The place was like my own mini Comic-Con! (You know, before the convention became more about TV shows and movies than comics. Blech.)

We paid the donation fee to the girl at the check-in desk and set out to explore. I showed Mom *Fables*, *Spider-Man Loves Mary Jane*, *Teen Titans*, and *The Avengers* and told her all about Marvel making Thor a girl in the comics. (Mom said I had lost my mind, but the girl at the desk backed me up.) I was practically floating by the time we reached the tiny gift shop on the way out. Immediately my eyes went to a poster that looked like Thor's hammer but was really made up of hundreds of tiny comic-book covers. I had to have it.

"Sorry, but he just bought the last two," the girl at the checkout told me regretfully.

Who had stolen my posters?

The girl pointed over my shoulder. I turned around and dropped my bag. "What are you doing here?"

Kyle was clutching two copies of my poster sheepishly. "Right, well, Jilly said there was a comic-book shop in town, and Heath and I felt we owed you a present for all your help with our homework and that nasty hotel fiasco in Nashville." He cleared his throat and side-eyed my mother. "So my brother brought me down to the store to find you something."

Kyle had come all this way to buy me a present? I noticed Kyle's older brother reading an *Ant-Man* comic a few aisles away. "That's so nice of you." Wow, this place really needed to invest in some air-conditioning!

Kyle was dressed in a vintage Beatles concert T-shirt, khaki shorts, and flip-flops. He looked like any other boy in my middle school, but for some reason I felt a knot form in my stomach when he started talking to Mom. "Hello, Piper," he said, sounding very proper, like we were out on a date and he was greeting my mom at the door.

OH MY GOD! I can't believe I just wrote that! WE WERE NOT ON A DATE!

Why would I even think that? And why was I suddenly staring at Kyle, wondering how he'd look in a jacket and tie? I'd seen him wear suits in music videos, but now I was imagining how he'd look in person all dressed up, ringing my doorbell, handing me flowers, and escorting me to my school dance. . . .

"Mac?" Mom and Kyle were looking at me strangely. "I said, this museum was worth the cab fare. You really liked it, right?"

Oh my God! What was I thinking? My apologies to Zander. "Yes! Sorry! Brain fart," I sputtered, my cheeks getting redder by the moment. I swear, I don't ever need to worry about wearing blush. I get embarrassed so often, my cheeks are pink all the time. "I'm surprised Heath didn't check out this place with you."

Kyle frowned. "He wanted to—which is why I got him a poster, too—but the mate never handed in his science paper to Krissy. She forced him to go back to the hotel after the event to get it done."

"That's too bad," Mom said. "You boys have been working so hard these last few weeks. Everyone needs a day off." Mom's phone was vibrating madly. When she looked at the caller ID, she made her internationally recognized gesture for *Must take this* (holding up one finger) and rushed to a quiet corner.

Kyle and I were alone. I could feel my palms begin to sweat. My chest felt itchy, like I had poison ivy, and I found myself staring an awfully long time at my beat-up sneakers. I listened to the muffled sounds of a video being played in the background and tried to concentrate on my breathing. What was happening to me?

"I'm sorry it's taking me so long to finish your song," Kyle said to break the silence.

"It's okay. You kind of have a lot going on," I tried to joke, but I felt nauseous.

"Well, I'm eighty-five percent done," Kyle said. "Not to be a total bragger, but Heath says the song is aces. I was playing it for him the other night, and he thinks it could actually be a single." He smiled. "You're like my own personal Yoko Ono."

I was Kyle's Yoko Ono? I giggled awkwardly and pulled at my T-shirt. It was starting to feel very tight. I was definitely getting a rash. "I'm glad to be of help." Without thinking, I looked up at him. Kyle was wearing a gray suit jacket and a red tie all of a sudden! I blinked. Now he was in a Beatles T-shirt and shorts again. I needed to get some air. "I should probably get Mom and get going. She's got a lot of work to do."

"Yes, blimey, she has her hands full!" Kyle said. "Zander was telling us about the Vegas pool party that's happening the week after next to announce the finalists of the contest."

"The contest?" I said weakly.

"Yeah, didn't your mum tell you? They're making a big announcement about that new fan contest. They're revealing the ten finalists on our website this evening, and then the top five will be named when we get to Vegas," Kyle told me, and I felt my blood run cold. "Briggs said girls have asked for everything from a concert at their prom to a date to their school dance."

Must. Not. Panic. People probably asked PS to school dances all the time.

"I almost forgot. This is for you." Kyle held a Thor poster out to me.

I gripped the tube tightly. "Thanks."

"Thank *you* for telling Briggs about my songs," Kyle said.

The funny thing was, it didn't feel like Kyle from PS had bought me the poster. Kyle the boy who liked songwriting and rhyming and playing the guitar had. The boy who loved sightseeing and could talk for hours about music and my artwork. The boy who was writing a song about me. The boy who . . .

I can't believe I'm writing this.

My hand is shaking as I hold the pen over the page.

The boy I want to go with me to my school dance.

Could I like Kyle Beyer?

I think I just might.

I'm supposed to be working on a paper about the Boston Tea Party while Krissy tests Heath on science stuff. (Krissy: "What is a black hole?" Heath: "What my hotel room smells like after I've had bean burritos.")

I'm glad Krissy is pulling her hair out with Heath, because I'm pulling my hair out about my accidental contest entry, which is sitting at the PS fan club and asks Zander to my school dance instead of Kyle. I've got to track it down so there's no chance of it ever making it into that contest, but how? What would alter-ego Mac do in this situation?

PS FAN CLUB
HEADQUARTERS.
MIDNIGHT.

CHKKY

PERFECT

CLICK!

I thought you'd be here.

You'll never find what you're looking for.

I want those lyrics you stole from me.

I thought I wanted to give them to you, but I changed my mind. I want to keep them for myself.

## Saturday, March 19

### LOCATION: Las Vegas, baby!

After a rocking show in Denver, Colorado, then a trip to Phoenix and a stop at Red Rock State Park for an Arizona magazine photo shoot, we went on to Las Vegas. When we stumbled off the tour bus at three AM, I barely noticed the hotel we were staying in (the Venetian), let alone what city we were in. So when I woke at eleven AM, I ran right to the window and threw open the shades to make sure I had my city right. LAS VEGAS! We were really here! I stared at the famous Las Vegas Strip I'd seen only in pictures. Bellagio's fountains; Paris Las Vegas, with its Eiffel Tower; New York-New York, with its mini city skyline

Bellagio Fountains

New York-New York

Paris

that reminded me of home. It was like I was visiting the whole world in one small city.

"Morning, sleepyhead!" Mom was putting on earrings as she emerged from the steamy bathroom in a beautiful black tank dress. "You slept like a true rocker."

"I know," I said with a satisfied sigh.

Mom sat at the edge of the bed and started to strap on her snakeskin heels. She had a very New York vibe going on. Mom always jokes you can tell the New York tour managers from the Los Angeles ones by the color they're wearing. New Yorkers always have on black, and Los Angelenos are more colorful. "So first things first, let's go over today's schedule."

"Okay." I turned toward her and tucked my bare feet under me, pulling on the edges of my pajama bottoms. The air-conditioning was turned up so high I thought I might become an ice sculpture. "Shoot!"

Mom had started giving me the rundown of her schedule before she left in the morning because her days were usually more hectic than she thought they'd be and sometimes I had no clue where she was. Or Mom would have a panic attack because I wasn't in our room, and it would turn out I was just down the hall in Jilly's room. So now we have Team Lowell meetings in the morning, and no one feels the need to call the police and file a missing person report (I wasn't thisclose to doing that in Texas. Nope! Not me!)

"I'll be with Briggs on the pool deck going over the PS pool party details with the hotel staff," Mom said.

My stomach began to hurt at the mere mention of the pool party. "Great! Super," I said, not worried at all. Not. At. All. "How are the finalists? Anyone from New York?" I asked nonchalantly.

"I can't remember," Mom said breezily. "I'm sure you'll find out at the party tomorrow night. The top five finalists will be announced there." She smiled. "Z100 has been so impressed with how the band's followers continue to rise that they've agreed to have PS on the morning show when we get back to New York. They'll pick the contest winner on the air!"

"Was there a Sabrina, by any chance?" I pressed. "I know a Sabrina who entered, so . . ."

"Your friend entered?" Mom asked. "That's so nice! I'll keep a lookout for the entry."

That's not what I wanted at all. I felt the panic bubbling over from the inside. "No, you don't have to—"

Mom cut me off. "Don't you want to hear what you'll be doing today? I know you like to plan your day, but I have a surprise."

"Is it a present?" I was momentarily distracted. I love presents! I looked around the room. I didn't see any wrapped boxes.

"I'm so proud of how you've been handling yourself on tour the last few weeks that I thought I'd give you the one thing you want more than anything in the world," Mom said.

"You already took me on tour with PS. What else could I want?" I gasped. "Are Scarlet and Iris coming to Las Vegas?"

Mom grinned and nodded. "They get in at three PM."

I can't even find a way to write down the

sound that came out of my mouth next. It was a combination of a fire alarm and a home security system that was accidentally tripped (I've set ours off once or twice). "THEY'RE COMING TODAY?"

Short answer: Yes.

The next few hours were a blur. I had to shower, make a welcome sign, and stalk the hotel lobby with Jilly for Scarlet and Iris's arrival. Mom sent a driver to pick them up at the airport and bring them right to the hotel, and then the next thing I knew, they were pulling up and I was jumping up and down. Scarlet and Iris got out of the car and started screaming, too, and Jilly started screaming supportively, and hotel security walked over and told us we had to keep it down. So we screamed quietly after that, while we all hugged and I made introductions. Scarlet and Jilly started talking about sporty things, because it turns out they both play softball (Is there a sport Jilly doesn't play?), while Iris brought me up to speed on the drama at our tae kwon do center. Riley Pierce had been bragging about going for her black belt, when we were sure she'd skipped a belt along the way.

Seconds later Scarlet grabbed me by the shoulders and looked me straight in the eyes. "Where are they? Did you tell them your friends were coming? Does Heath know my name?"

Iris swatted her. "Scar! We haven't even had time to catch up with Mac yet. PS can wait." Iris's right eye started to twitch, which was how I knew she was lying. "Although, if you wanted to get the introductions over with, that would be okay, too. I know Zander is yours, but . . ."

"Zander is not mine," I said quickly.

" . . . I still want to meet him," Iris went on, not hearing me. "I'm happy for you, and I know I'll find my own Zander someday, or maybe, who knows? You'll be with Zander, and Scarlet will be with Heath, and maybe I'll like Kyle," she said brightly.

"No!" I blurted out. Scarlet and Iris looked at me strangely. "I just mean, Kyle is really funny and sensitive, while Zander is more about his work and his fans and . . ."

Iris and Scarlet looked from me to Jilly for help. She shrugged. "Kyle and Mac like each other. They just don't seem to realize it yet."

"Who wants to go on a gondola ride?" I suggested loudly, forgetting we were in a large Las Vegas lobby with loads of people and crazy acoustics. The floors were marble, and there was a river that ran through the hotel. "They look like fun."

"A boat ride can wait." Scarlet unbuttoned her sweater to reveal a HEATH CAN'T BE BEAT T-shirt. "What's up with you and Kyle? What happened to Zander? And more importantly, can I meet Heath? PLEASE, Mac? PLEASE?" Scarlet never begged.

Jilly started to laugh. "Mac, they sound just like you did when you first got on the road. Let's

236

drop off their luggage and find Mikey G. to see where the guys are."

Note to self: If you're ever wondering where a boy is, the first thing you should think about is food. Boys are always hungry.

Zander, Kyle, and Heath were having a mini meeting with Briggs in the Venetian's food court. They had a whole section to themselves, since Mikey G. was blocking a group of girls from trying to make their way to the table. Cell phones were held high in the air to take the guys' pictures.

Iris dug her nails into my bare arm and squealed. "OhmyGodthat'sZanderrightthereat thattableandhe'seatingnongreenfood!"

Zander looked up and grinned. "Hey, Mac. Jilly. Ladies. You must be Mac's friends."

Iris pushed past me. "WemetinNewYorkback stageatSongSlammynameisIris." She giggled uncontrollably as Zander walked over and pulled her in for a hug.

"Nice to see you again, Iris," Zander said. He was wearing a vintage Studio B tee he got in Nashville. "You have amazing brown eyes. They look like Nesquik syrup."

"I love Nesquik syrup!" Iris gushed.

I wasn't sure I'd ever seen Iris swig chocolate milk in her life, but whatever.

"So are you girls sitting in the VIP area for the show tomorrow night?" Zander asked. "Mac got you seats, didn't she?"

"I didn't know if there were VIP tickets left," I admitted. "The last two shows I've had to watch from the backstage monitor because Lola Cummings had so many guests."

Jilly, Scarlet, and Iris scowled as any good friend would at the mention of someone's mortal enemy.

"Well, I'll tell Lola she has four less tickets for the Hard Rock show," Zander said. "Iris and Scarlet deserve the best seats in the house if one of them is going to be called onstage during 'I Feel Blue.'"

Iris gasped.

"You guys have heard how well it's doing, right? One of the top fifty downloads on iTunes right now."

"We just knew PS was going to be famous!" Iris squealed. "We've been fans forever!"

"I love hearing that." Zander grinned. "And if that's the case, maybe you can help us." He put an arm around each of them and led them to the

239

table. "We're trying to narrow down the finalists in this contest we're running."

"We have to pick five from these ten," Briggs said. "But the boys can't seem to agree on any of their picks."

"I can't help it," Heath protested. "I like the girl who wants to take me to her dad's tattoo parlor to get matching tattoos and talk about ink life."

"You don't really want a girl to pick out a tattoo for you," Briggs said. "Believe me."

"She might make you get one of Tigger," Zander teased.

Heath looked at him darkly. "Why would you bring up Tigger in front of the girls?"

"What?" Zander said, widening his eyes to look innocent. "I'm just saying I don't know any other guys who sleep with a stuffed animal at our age."

Heath didn't think this was funny. He pushed back his chair and began loading everyone's garbage onto his tray. Scarlet sighed. I knew what she was thinking—she's a neat freak, so watching Heath go out of his way to clean something up was making her swoon. I wasn't going to tell her about the whipped-cream fight in Nashville or how messy his bunk bed was. "I'm not hungry anymore," Heath grumbled. "Forget the tattoo entry. Just go with the prom one that Zander wants. We always pick his choice anyway."

Prom? Prom was different from Spring Fling, right?

"We do not." Zander looked at Briggs. "I was just making a funny, man. Geez, can't the guy take a joke? I mean, he does wear fake tattoo sleeves."

Scarlet gasped and looked at Jilly and me. "They're fake?"

We nodded sadly. I had forgotten to tell her before now. Scarlet recovered quickly when she realized Heath was about to walk past us.

"Heath?" He turned around and noticed her HEATH CAN'T BE BEAT T-shirt. "I just wanted to say that your real fans don't care whether you have tattoos or not, or if you sleep with a stuffed animal. We like you for you."

*We like you for you.*

Heath pulled Scarlet in for a bear hug. Iris snapped a picture with her phone, Jilly smiled, and I thought about what Scarlet had just said. I would never have said this to my best friends, but before I went on the road with Perfect Storm, all we'd really known about PS was what they wanted us to know. In real life they were very different from their YouTube videos. They were funnier, smarter, louder, and quirkier. They liked things they didn't share with the world, like stuffed tigers, songwriting, and caring a lot about their careers. They were goofy boys who talked about farting, boogers, and burps. Heath had become like the brother I didn't have,

Zander was the business brains whom I wanted to win over the world, and Kyle . . . well, Kyle was way different than I'd ever imagined.

"Zander! Heath! Kyle!" The chants of the girls standing mere feet away pulled me back from my thoughts. Girls were finding the guys more and more these days.

"Well, I should spread the love," Zander said. "I'll see you ladies later. We should definitely do dinner!" I thought Iris's face was going to burst into flames, it was so red. "I'll text you, Mac. Bye, Jilly Bean."

After one more hug from Heath, who claimed he had to head to the gym (he never goes to the gym, FYI), Scarlet and Iris were practically Jell-O.

"They're amazing," Iris said in a dreamy voice. "Even more amazing than the amazingness that I was sure they were going to be! And Zander is getting us VIP seats to tomorrow night's show!" Iris started to boogie in the middle of the food

243

court, and an elderly couple wearing WE GOT HITCHED IN VEGAS IN '64 tees took their trays to the other side of the room. "Mac, why didn't you tell us they were this amazing?"

And then Kyle walked up to us. "I just wanted to properly introduce myself to Mac's mates." He shook hands with Scarlet and Iris, who looked gobsmacked. "Piper told me she was surprising Mac with a visit from you two. It's good to meet you both."

"He speaks," Iris said.

Kyle laughed. "Yes, I speak. So let's see if I can guess who is who." Kyle stepped back and

244

framed both girls' faces with his hands. He pointed to Iris. "You're Iris. I can tell because Mac said you take tae kwon do together. Your hands are in this karate-chop position right now, so I'm going to move back."

"Sorry!" Iris said with a laugh. "I get in self-defense mode when I'm nervous. That was awesome! I can't believe you knew who was who."

"And, Scarlet, you are the one who plays softball, right?" Kyle asked. "Mac said you're going to be captain next year. That's brill."

"Brill," Scarlet repeated, as if in a fog. I understood. It was hard not to fall for Kyle's accent. She quickly snapped out of it. "Well, I want to be captain, but there is fierce competition, so we'll have to see."

Kyle nodded and looked at me. "I was going to see if you wanted to go on a gondola ride and then maybe head over to New York-New York to ride the coaster. Mikey G. says it's on the roof!

We don't have anything tonight, so I thought I'd fancy a look around town." His expression changed when he looked at Iris and Scarlet. "But I'm sure you want to do touristy things with your mates now that they're here."

"Come with us," Iris said, taking the words right out of my mouth.

I seriously have the best friends in the world.

# Sunday, March 20
## (It's so early, it's still the middle of the night!)

## LOCATION: Sleepover party in Jilly's room in Vegas!

Here's the cool thing about having a dad who is a millionaire. When he sees his daughter having fun with a bunch of girls her own age, he gets her a suite for the night so she can have a sleepover party. We were even allowed to order room service!

Briggsy seriously is the best.

The bathroom is bigger than my room at home. The tub is the size of the Jacuzzi in Iris's backyard. We even have our own living room with a flat-screen TV where we can rent pretty much any movie we can think of! I'm happy Jilly fit into our little group despite the fact that she is not a PS fanatic like the rest of us. When she started acting out scenes from *Life After Life*, Iris laughed so hard, fruit punch came out of her nose.

"Let's play truth or dare," Scarlet suggested as she brushed her hair and put rollers in it. The four of us had decided we were going to go Las Vegas glam for the concert later that night.

"I hate truth or dare," I whined as I painted my toenails a wicked shade of hot pink.

"That's because you always hate doing the dares," Scarlet said. "Ooh, Mac, is that pink on your nails? What happened to red?"

I had painted my toenails red ever since we learned red was Zander's favorite color. But tonight, when Jilly broke out her nail polishes, I was drawn to the pink one. Huh. "I just wanted something different, I guess."

"While you're being bold, I say you go first," Scarlet challenged, her eyes blazing in the glow of the TV in the darkened room. We had moved our pillows and blankets onto the floor of the living room after Iris protested that the mattresses in hotel rooms all had bed bugs and we couldn't use them. Then Scarlet said that if the comforters had bed bugs, then the sheets did, too. Jilly said the sheets were washed daily, so we settled on sleeping on sheets. "So, truth or dare?"

I bit my lip. The last time I picked dare, Scarlet had made me run down the block in my pajamas wearing a shark-head mask. I tripped

251

over a skateboard and got three stitches in my knee. I did not want any more stitches. "Truth."

The girls leaned forward. Jilly started to laugh wildly. We were hopped up on candy, so anything we said sounded funny at this point. "Do you like Zander or do you like Kyle?" Scarlet wanted to know. "Because, Mac, we love you, and the way you and Kyle were chatting at New

York-New York this afternoon, and then how you had to sit next to him in the front seat of the coaster, and how he challenged you to an ice-cream-eating contest at dinner at the buffet . . . I don't know. It seems like you like Kyle. So do you?"

I looked at my friends. In the background our fourth movie had just started, and I could see a girl running from the Sharkinator as it attacked her on the beach. My heart was beating out of my chest, and my throat felt dry and scratchy. Possibly because I was nervous and possibly because it was raw from all that sugar in the gummy candies I had just eaten.

"I think so," I said finally.

My friends screamed. Seconds later someone pounded on the floor above us.

"I knew it!" Iris said. "And, Mac, I'm not just saying this as someone who has always loved Zander as much as you do—I like you liking Kyle. He's so much cooler than we thought he was."

253

"I know!" I munched on more candy happily.

"Are you going to tell him?" Scarlet asked excitedly. "Or are you going to draw him an album cover or write him a poem? You love writing poems with PS song lyrics. Ooh! You should do that."

The contest. I had almost forgotten about it. My half-eaten gummy fell out of my mouth.

"EWW!" the girls screamed at the same time. More pounding came from the ceiling.

"Guys, hotel security is going to come up here if we don't quiet down," Jilly said. "Mac, what is wrong with you? You just wasted a perfectly good piece of candy."

"I couldn't help it. It's just . . . I did something I'm worried is going to bite me big-time." I sounded like a character on *Life After Life*.

Iris's eyes widened. "What did you do?"

My face burned. I mean, who wrote fan mail anymore when you could just tweet a band? "Before my mom told me about going on tour, I wrote Zander a poem with PS lyrics and asked him to our school dance." I covered my face with my hands.

Scarlet burst out laughing, and both Jilly and Iris hit her.

"It's not funny!" I cried. "What if my fan mail makes it into the contest? Tomorrow night is the big pool party to announce the five finalists."

"Mac, no offense, but there are probably thousands of entries," Jilly said. "Even if Daddy found yours, he wouldn't and couldn't use it because it's against the rules to pick an entry from someone working with the band. You're in the clear."

"Maybe not." I looked at the nail polish bottle in my hand and watched the pink swish back and forth. I spoke really fast because I was so nervous. "My mom says no dating till high school, so I freaked out that Zander would get the poster and fall madly in love with me, and I wouldn't be able to go to the dance with him because of

255

my mom! So I signed the poster with my middle name and created a fake e-mail account for him to contact me at."

"MAC!" Scarlet was gobsmacked. "That's genius. And bad. And genius! Have you looked at the e-mail account to see if you've heard anything about the contest?" I shook my head. "Then we have to look at it RIGHT. NOW!"

"Yeah, but aren't *winners* the only ones notified of winning a contest?" Iris pointed out. "I've never been notified, 'Hey, good try, but you actually lost.'"

Scarlet gave her a look. "We should still check! Briggs said they were narrowing down the finalists. Maybe they let them know they were in the top five. Let's look."

Scarlet and Jilly dived over the pillows and went scrambling for the first tablet they could find. It was Scarlet's. I could tell by the furry red cover with the letter H on it for "Heath." They fired it up.

"What e-mail account did you use?" Jilly asked.

It had been so long, I could hardly remember. I thought for a moment. "It would be SabrinalovesZ@yahoo.com." I could picture the screen in my mind. "My password is always ZanderGirl5 so that's got to be the password." We watched as the e-mail account began to load.

Ten seconds had never felt so long in my life!

"We're in!" Jilly announced.

Scarlet's and Jilly's eyes ran down the page. Iris tried to see over their shoulders, but I stayed back. I was too nervous to look. There was no way I'd been chosen, but what if? WHAT IF? How would I explain myself to Mom? To Briggs? To Zander?

To Kyle?

"Oooh!" Jilly gasped.

"What is it?" I freaked out, grabbing Iris and holding on tight.

"Sabrina has two twenty-five-percent-off

257

coupons!" Jilly announced, and I glared at her. "That and a few spam e-mails are all that's there. You're in the clear!"

We cheered—quietly, though, so that hotel security wouldn't be called—and I felt this huge knot in my neck suddenly disappear. Iris still looked worried. I tried not to look at her.

"This calls for an ice-cream sundae bar." Jilly went to the phone and dialed room service.

Everyone started calling out flavors and toppings, but I didn't care what we ordered. I was just happy that I was not going to win the contest.

I might not even be home for the Spring Fling. Lemon Ade had already asked the guys to do ten more dates on her tour, taking them through the end of April. Briggs said at this rate the boys would have their own headlining tour by the summer! Now that this silly contest wasn't hanging over me, my new life could stay exactly as it was—zanily, crazily wonderful.

I was cool with that.

## Sunday, March 20

"Thisconcertisamazing!" Iris said so quickly it came out as one long word. She had to shout to be heard over Lemon Ade's set, which had just started.  "Istillcan'tbelievewe'reintheVIPareafor theLemonAde/PSconcert!"

Tonight's concert seats were off the hook. I couldn't believe Zander was able to score us VIP tickets. There were so many record label people in from L.A. for the PS party following the concert that every seat was taken. Even Lola Cummings was resigned to the back row of our tiny, roped-off section near the stage. I actually turned around at one point and waved to her. She made a motion to me that I'd rather not repeat.

"I really don't like that girl," Scarlet said, even though this was the first time she had ever seen Lola in person. I guess Jilly and I had described her well enough that Scarlet could spot her in a crowd and hate her on sight. That's what good friends are for.

And then before we knew it, Lemon Ade was running offstage to rev up the crowd to ask for an encore. The place was stomping, clapping, and screaming, and our ears were ringing. Lemon Ade emerged from the ceiling on a tire swing, wearing this sequined two-piece outfit. I wondered if Mac in *Mac Attack* could pull off an outfit like that one.

"I'd like to welcome back my favorite boys in the world to help me out on my number 'Boys' Club,'" Lemon Ade told the crowd. "PS, soon to be the biggest band on the planet!"

And there they were again—Zander, Heath, and Kyle, looking fresh in new clothes. Lemon Ade had never called them out for an encore before, but it was a good idea because the crowd was going wild for PS.

Scarlet practically cried when they came back onstage. "First it was eighth-place slots in state fairs, and now our boys are opening for Lemon Ade." She squeezed me. "Your mom must be a genius tour manager!"

Before we knew it, our ears were ringing louder than ever, the lights were coming up, and we were being herded like cattle out of the concert hall and back into the even brighter casino, where slots whirling and machines beeping sounded like a symphony. It was time for the PS after-concert pool party and the contest winner announcement. For the first time in weeks I didn't care who won. I knew it wouldn't be me!

Up, up, up we flew in one of the glass

elevators, talking a mile a minute about Lemon Ade's wardrobe ("I heard it's worth almost a million dollars," Scarlet said), the best PS number of the night ("'I Need You' will always be my favorite PS song," Iris said), and what kind of food was going to be at this party ("I begged Daddy to order mini hot dogs even if they're not very chic," Jilly revealed). And then the doors to the rooftop party opened, and we were speechless.

"Whoa," Jilly said first.

"Double whoa," Scarlet repeated.

The Las Vegas skyline spread out beyond the roof, where palm trees swayed and a lit-up bar was serving smoothies as well as drinks I couldn't touch. The illuminated pool was open and full of guitar-shaped floats, but no one was swimming. This crowd did not look like pool types. They were dressed in sequins, high heels, and lots of jewelry, and suddenly I felt silly in my favorite-ever red sundress, which had a scalloped edge right above my knees. Alter-ego Mac would have worn something rocker cool like a pink leather miniskirt and a tank top that said MUSIC IS MY SUPERPOWER.

"I can't believe they let children into this party."

There was only one person who would say that. "Hi, Lola," I said wearily. She had Bridget and the babysitter she didn't call a babysitter with her. They both had on outfits very similar to what my alter ego would wear. But they didn't look like they were playing dress-up like I would have.

Lola pretended to yawn, her high-gloss pink lips smacking as she talked. "What are you doing here? Isn't it past your bedtime?"

"We're not the ones who look like we need our beauty sleep," Scarlet said, stepping slightly in front of me, her arms across her chest, hiding her PS, WE WILL LOVE YOU FOREVER AND EVER AND EVER shirt I designed for the three of us last fall. Both she and Iris had theirs on with skirts. She motioned to Lola's eyes. "Nice dark circles. We don't have those yet. We're not old like you." Iris, Jilly, and I giggled.

Lola stared at us blankly, as if she couldn't believe someone our age could come up with a comeback that fierce. For a moment one of her fake eyelashes seemed to glue itself to her lower

266

lid, and she had to rub her eye to get it to come undone. "I should go," Lola sniffed, snapping her fingers to get her babysitter and Bridget to follow. "Zander is probably looking for me. He's texted me twice."

"Ugh!" Iris said when Lola was gone. "She's worse than you described."

"I know," I said, but for some reason she didn't bother me as much as she usually did.

"You ladies look like you're up to no good." Kyle appeared in the crowd. He gave Scarlet a hug. "What are you plotting? Taking over the world?"

"Love him," Iris mouthed when Kyle hugged her.

"Just the hotel," Scarlet said cheerfully. "Your show tonight was amazing! I loved when you guys sang your new single. That guitar solo you did was unbelievable."

Kyle's face flushed slightly. "Zander actually broke his mic, so I had to improvise till he could

267

run offstage and get a new one, hence the guitar solo."

"I didn't even see him leave the stage," I realized. Jilly and Scarlet coughed, and Iris sneezed.

"Gesundheit," Kyle said.

"Gesundheit?" I laughed. "Who says that?" We all laughed.

Kyle nudged me and I nudged him back—right into a waiter carrying appetizers.

"Ooh! Mini hot dogs!" Scarlet snagged two. We all started grabbing, and the waiter's tray was empty by the time he walked away.

"Good evening, everyone." Briggs was standing near the back of the pool, where a microphone was set up. "I want to thank you for coming tonight to celebrate the success of PS." The crowd roared with approval.

"I should go," Kyle said. "We're announcing the contest finalists. You guys are staying, right?" We nodded and Kyle smiled. "Okay. Cheers, then. I'll see you in a few."

"Yep, he likes you," Iris whispered when Kyle walked away.

"I'd like to get the party started with some exciting news about Perfect Storm," Briggs said as the band approached the mic. Mom was standing alongside Briggs in a beautiful green silk dress. "Lemon Ade has asked the band to stay on till the end of the tour as her opening act!" The party guests broke into applause. Kyle, Zander, and Heath did the "bro" hug. "Hopefully this is the first of many tours you'll catch the boys on, especially now that they've been named one of Wave One's Top Bands to Watch." Lola was standing behind Briggs, and her big blond hair flew up and down at the announcement.

"Wave One has been so generous to the band, as has Z100, who has invited the boys to debut their new single and appear on the famous morning show."

Jilly and I looked at each other. Way to go,

Mom! No wonder she was smiling. She saw me watching her and gave a little wink.

"And now we'd like to announce the top five finalists of the PS Fan Moment Contest," Briggs said. "They'll be invited to meet the band in New York, and the official winner will be announced on-air."

"Wow, that's so cool! I wish I entered," Iris said with a sigh.

Scarlet nudged her. "Dude, you're here with them now."

Who cared who won? I stared at Kyle, watching him grin and laugh at something Heath said. I expected my mind to go into future-Mac mode, like it always did with Zander, but strangely, I didn't see Kyle and me on a beach. I saw us here, on the road, side by side, doing homework on his tour bus. That could actually happen. Tomorrow, even, on the way to L.A. I felt goose bumps on my arms and rubbed them to keep warm.

"I will now turn it over to Perfect Storm to announce their favorites," Briggs said.

Girls screamed as Zander took the mic. He pushed his mop of hair out of his eyes and gave that million-watt grin that had always reduced me to a puddle. "How you doing, Las Vegas?" he asked the crowd, who went wild. "Perfect Storm is very excited about this contest that is all about our dedicated fans. We've spent hours and weeks narrowing down five entries from thousands."

"You mean Daddy and Piper narrowed down and gave you a few choices," Jilly whispered in my ear.

"Kyle will share the first one," Zander said.

I watched Kyle take the mic and wondered suddenly what Kyle's winning entry would be about.

"Evening. My heart belongs to one pick only. TabbyCat87, who asked Perfect Storm to help her with her Habitat for Humanity project in Alabama. She'll be building a home for a family that lost everything in a tornado this past fall, and

271

she thought having the band help build would cheer up the nine-year-old in the family who lost all her possessions. I couldn't agree more," Kyle said.

"He is so deep." Scarlet clutched her heart. "He is my new second-favorite member."

"Heath here! Rock on, Vegas! My top two pics—and yes, there are two—include Reeses-Pieces, who is trying to save her inner-city park from turning into a convenience store. She is hoping a benefit performance from PS will help raise awareness. I'm in," he said, and held up a tattoo-sleeved arm to rally the audience. Then Heath grinned wickedly. "My second pick is more selfish." Everyone laughed. "TinyDancer45 wants to take me and the guys to Disney World as dates to her sister's wedding. Sounds like fun to me!"

"And here are my two picks," Zander told the audience as he grabbed the mic from Heath. I took two mini quiches off a tray and munched happily. I finally had my appetite back. "First off is a YouTube video from StarryEyedPSGirl. She is suggesting that PS take over a cruise ship and do a benefit concert on board, with all money raised going to our favorite charity. She, of course, would like a room on the ship because it was her suggestion." The audience laughed. "I could use a tan, so this sounds good to me! My second choice is Sabrina from New York, who created this stellar drawing of Perfect Storm along with a poem asking me to her first middle school dance. Let me read it to you."

I dropped my second mini quiche on the floor.

Jilly, Scarlet, and Iris spun their heads around so fast they looked like that girl in *The Exorcist* (which I have seen only in clips on TV, because that movie is way too scary to watch—just like this moment was turning out to be way too scary to live through).

"Is that yours?" Jilly asked as Zander read

a particularly painful line about needing him more than a fish needed water. I nodded.

Blood. Draining. From. My. Face.

"But how?" Scarlet asked. "We checked Yahoo! We checked the spam. There was nothing. . . ."

Jilly slapped her head. "We're such idiots. Of course there's no e-mail yet. They're probably calling or e-mailing the winners now."

Iris nudged me. "Check that e-mail address again! Now!"

"I can't," I said. "My hands are shaking." I felt numb and heard a whooshing sound in my ears. "You do it."

Both Scarlet and Jilly went straight to their phones and pulled up Yahoo! Within seconds, they looked from each other to me. "Sabrina has an e-mail from the Perfect Storm fan club," Scarlet said nervously. Jilly held out the phone for me to read it.

Sabrina—

Congratulations! You have been selected
as a finalist in the PS Fan Moment Contest
and have been invited to meet the band
in New York. Please contact the firm of
Zwanger and Wilder as soon as possible.
They will go over all contest paperwork
and make travel arrangements for you
and a guardian.

Good luck, and know that Perfect Storm
loves you!

—The PS We Love You Official Fan Club

"That drawing is wicked," Heath was saying
as Zander held up my entry for the whole roof
to see. "Look at the detail on my face. This chick
can draw."

Kyle leaned in to give the poster a closer look, and I held my breath. "She certainly can. The artwork looks kind of familiar, actually."

Aah! Kyle was going to figure this out.

I had the sudden urge to become alter-ego Mac and rappel off the side of the building, using the velvet rope behind the pool as a climbing device.

"We'll now take a few questions from reporters in the audience," I heard Mom say, and I was never so grateful to hear my mother interrupt a conversation before.

"We were wondering if you guys had a favorite entry yet," someone said.

Zander looked at my mom. "Well, obviously I can't say, other than that all five girls' entries are winners in my heart." I heard a collective "awww." "But if I had my choice, it would be Sabrina. I want to meet the girl who can draw me looking like a Greek god."

Kyle ran his finger along the poster. My heart was beating out of my chest.

"Of course you want to win," Heath teased, but there was an edge to his voice. "You *always* want to win the top prize. I say go for the girl who wants all of us to go to Disney World. Now, that sounds like fun. Not you as a solo act at some middle school dance."

"Disney World!" Zander snorted. "Can you

believe this guy? I guess I shouldn't be surprised. He sleeps with a Tigger stuffed animal on the tour bus!" The audience laughed. Heath looked ready to smash something.

"Oh yeah? Well, this guy sleeps with a night-light in his hotel room!" Heath shot back, then kept going. "And the real reason he doesn't ride escalators isn't because he lost part of a toe in an accident. It's because he's afraid of how fast the steps are moving!"

Zander's eyes nearly bulged out of his head.

"Um, guys?" Kyle started to say. My mom tried to grab the mic.

"Your tattoos are fake!" Zander blurted out. "He wears tattoo sleeves."

"You watch *Bubble Guppies*!" Heath shouted.

"So do you!" Zander fired back. "And *Life After Life*."

I pictured Mac Attack halfway down the side of the building and hearing this fight break out. She'd probably find a way to climb back up the

building and then use that velvet rope to tie up the boys till they stopped fighting. But I just stood there watching the train wreck.

"I don't need this crap," Heath hollered. "I'm out of here!"

"Good! You can easily be replaced," Zander shouted.

"Breakup alert! Breakup alert!" Scarlet freaked out.

Iris grabbed my arm as Heath pulled back his own and prepared to deck Zander. Thankfully,

Mom stepped in just in time and took a jab to her right arm. She did not look thrilled as she pulled the boys offstage and away from the party.

Neither did Briggs as he quickly took the mic and said, "Are those three hams or what?" He gave a fake laugh. "We'll have more details on the Perfect Storm Fan Moment Contest on the band's website later this evening. For further questions"—people in the audience started raising their hands—"please contact the band's label publicist, Megan Earles. Thank you, and enjoy the mini hot dogs. They're out of this world!" Then he ran off the stage.

From a distance I could see Mom herding the guys into an elevator. They were still yelling at each other. I thought Kyle made eye contact with me, but the doors closed.

"Um, guys?" Iris sounded nervous. "Did our favorite band just break up?"

The four of us looked at each other. We were too afraid to answer.

# Tuesday, March 22

## LOCATION: Los Angeles, California, city of broken dreams

Yes, I know I sound miserable, but I have a good reason.

I think my poster just broke up Perfect Storm!

The sun was shining brightly outside our hotel room window, and the day off meant Universal Studios was calling our names, but we could barely muster the energy to brush our teeth, let alone leave the room. That was pretty sad because Iris and Scarlet were still with us, and the three of us had never been to Los Angeles before. We had changed Iris and Scarlet's flight home after the PS Fight Heard Round the World. Iris told her mom that it was a "life-or-death emergency that

Mac needed help with," and thankfully, Mom backed that up with a phone call to her as well. I have no idea what she said, but it was somehow enough to convince Iris's mom (who thinks our love of PS is a phase) to let her stay on for a few more days, since it was still their spring break.

"Another tweet coming in," Jilly announced as we sat huddled together on my bed. "Pop-Wrapped says: 'Did Perfect Storm implode before they ever got off the ground?' And then there is an article link." Jilly opened it up and groaned. "Another eyewitness of the party."

"Half these people weren't even AT the party," Scarlet barked. "A girl on Instagram claims she has a photo of Heath and Zander hitting each other, but I KNOW this picture was taken from their YouTube channel skit they did last May called 'Boys Gone Wild,' so HA!" Scarlet's hair looked like a tornado had gone through it. None of us had unpacked our bags or knew where a comb was.

"No word from your mom?" Iris asked tear-fully.

"I've barely talked to her since Las Vegas," I said. "She is in crisis mode."

She even rode a separate tour bus from me. My mom said only Kyle was on it. Heath and Zander both got rides from other people to L.A. to avoid each other.

"I keep telling her that we need to talk privately, but she is too busy to. I need to tell her that I'm really Sabrina, so I can get my entry disqualified."

"I wouldn't bother," Scarlet said dejectedly. "It looks like the band is breaking up anyway."

"And it's all my fault," I whispered.

I had tried texting Kyle to see if he was okay, but he hadn't replied. I knew he had a lot going on, but I was still worried about him. Was he as mad as the others? Did he know that Sabrina was really me? "Have you heard from Briggs?" I asked Jilly.

She shook her head. "I've been texting and texting and getting no reply. His assistant is the only one talking, and it's just to give me updates on where Dad is—a meeting, another meeting, and a third meeting with Piper and the label publicists."

"Another tweet!" Scarlet groaned. "This one is from someone who says she knows someone who is best friends with Zander, and Zander is going to go solo."

We took in the news silently.

Yes, Zander was the face of the band. And sure, he had the voice of an angel. Other boy bands had broken up and their lead singer had gone on to be big (hi, Justin Timberlake!), but Perfect Storm was different. Everyone in the room knew it. Heath made the group fun, Kyle gave the group heart, and Zander was their voice. PS wouldn't feel the same if there was just an S. They worked only when they were together. I wondered if they knew that.

"We have to talk to them," I said suddenly.

Iris sprang up. She was still clutching my stuffed monkey. "Okay! Yes! Talk to them! What are we going to say?"

"We're going to tell them they're all big-headed idiots who are going to ruin their lives if they don't get over this stupid fight," Scarlet said. We looked at her. "Well, we won't say it like that. We'll say it nicely."

"How are we going to get them in the same room?" Iris asked. "You heard Jilly—their managers and a team of publicists can't pull that off. How are we going to?"

287

Mac Attack could pull this off. I had to think like I was living in my comic book. That Mac would tell the boys exactly what Scarlet just said, even if she had to do it by holding them all hostage. That gave me an idea. "Jilly, do you think you could get Lemon Ade to send a text for us?"

"Why?" Jilly bit on a pencil she had in her hand.

"Well, maybe the boys won't talk to each other, and they won't talk to Briggs or my mom, but maybe if they *each* think Lemon Ade wants to talk to them about opening as a solo artist, they'd show up."

"You want to lie to them?" Iris's eyes bulged out of her head.

"Yes!" I said as Scarlet's phone pinged with more Twitter updates. "This could be our one shot to get the guys on the same page before they do something stupid and break up."

"And ruin our lives," Iris seconded.

"You can beg your dad's assistant to help us," I suggested to Jilly. "We're really doing this for Lemon Ade, when you think about it. She needs the guys to stay on the tour because they're selling tickets." I thought for a moment. "You can tell Lemon Ade you're texting for your dad because his phone died."

Jilly shrugged. "It's worth a shot."

"Another lie?" Iris cried. "We are going to get in so much trouble if this doesn't work."

Jilly's fingers flew over her cell phone, and within minutes Briggs's assistant sent us the number and Jilly sent Lemon Ade a text. Ten torturous minutes later Lemon Ade texted her back and agreed to be part of our plan (as long as this never came up in the press—pop stars are so touchy). We agreed and had her send the boys a text asking them to meet in what was really Jilly's suite that afternoon at 2:45, 2:48, and 2:50 PM, and hoped they weren't suspicious about the strange arrival times.

"She says they all said yes," Jilly shared. We all cheered.

I took a deep breath and looked at the others. "Let's do this!"

A little while later we were waiting in the bedroom of Jilly's suite when a bewildered Kyle walked in with Mikey G., who we had recruited for our scheme as well. He told the boys he was working security for Lemon Ade for the day, since her main bodyguard was sick. Kyle had bought it. Two minutes later, and on time for a change, Heath strolled in. When he first saw Kyle, he froze, but then I heard him say, "I have no real beef with you, man."

"Same here, mate," Kyle said. "This fight is totally bollocks."

And then the two shook hands!

Scarlet, Iris, and I group-hugged. Look at that! One fight was over, and we didn't have to do a thing but get them in the same room. Then there was a third knock at the door, and Zander strode in in a cloud of maple-syrup-smelling cologne.

"What the . . . ," he started to say when he saw Kyle and Heath. "I'm out of here."

That's when Jilly, Iris, Scarlet, and I jumped out from our hiding place and stood in front of him. It felt very Mac Attack, which was so cool.

"Go sit down now, Z.," Mikey G. said in his most menacing bodyguard voice. "And if you ever knock Life After Life again, you and I are going to have to have a talk." Mikey G. and I high-fived, and I handed him our leftover candy as promised.

Zander dragged himself to a chair near the couch and folded his arms across his chest. "This is not right," he said and pouted. "I have nothing to say to him."

"And I have nothing to say to you," Heath shot back. "Dude, how could you tell people my tats are fake?"

"How could you tell people I made up that escalator story?" Zander asked.

"Why do you guys go crazy over this stuff?" Kyle chimed in, and then the three of them were throwing insults at each other and yelling, and Zander was threatening to walk out again, and I screamed, "STOP!"

Zander sat right back down, and the three of

them looked at me. They actually seemed frightened. Maybe I could channel my alter ego, Mac Attack, after all.

"Thank you," I said more calmly. I looked at Scarlet and Iris, who encouraged me to go on. Jilly appeared at my side. "The reason we lied to get you in the same room is we don't want to see you guys break up." None of them looked convinced. "You three belong together like Nutella and frozen bananas." They still weren't moved. "You've come so far. Do you really want to back out now?" No answer.

Scarlet sighed. Iris looked teary. Jilly pursed her lips and put her hands on her hips, and I knew what she was thinking: We weren't going to get anywhere. Briggs hadn't. My mom hadn't. We weren't going to, either. And that made me mad.

"You know what? Fine! Break up! See if we care. Another band will be along in five minutes to take your place." For the first time they looked

293

up at me. "You'll never get a major album. You'll never be on late-night TV. You'll never head-line your own tour. You can all go back to doing what you were doing before you became Perfect Storm, because Lemon Ade is not going to hire any of you to be her opening act on your own."

Okay, I didn't know that for sure, but I needed to say something that would scare them. I thought of what alter-ego Mac would say (before she went off to fight crime) and decided to go with my gut.

"Jilly has spent the last year on the road with you guys, and her dad has spent longer than that putting your group together," I reminded them. "People have spent a lot of time and money on you three because they believe you can be stars. Now you're all about to throw it away because of some stupid fight about *Bubble Guppies* and Tig-ger?" Kyle winced. "Scarlet, Iris, and I have loved you guys from the first time we heard you sing. We've spent hours tweeting you, liking your

YouTube posts, requesting you on the radio, and telling everyone we know what a great band you are. There are thousands of other girls out there who adore you, too." I looked at my friends. "Real friends know how to put each other first. You guys need to do the same in your group. Perfect Storm doesn't work if you're not all in it."

The room was quiet for a moment. House-keeping actually knocked on the door.

"Do not disturb," Mikey G. said gruffly.

The boys didn't move. Heath played with his T-shirt. I noticed he wasn't wearing his tattoo sleeves. Zander stared at the ceiling. Kyle looked pained. Iris was visibly teary. I guess the only one my speech had made an impact on was her.

Then Heath turned to Zander. "Dude, no one is saying you should stop being the face of the band. The girls like your hair too much for that to happen." Zander kind of smiled. "We're just asking you to share the spotlight sometimes."

"You guys don't get it," Zander said. "All I have

is my voice and my hair. Kyle writes and plays the guitar. You play the guitar and the drums. I'm just a puppet with a microphone."

"So what?" Heath said. "A lot of stars out there can't do anything but sing." He paused. "And you do so much more than that. If it weren't for you, the band wouldn't have half the followers we have. You're a social-media god. The girls love you."

"That they do." Zander winked at us. We all groaned.

Heath and Zander looked at Kyle. "I didn't have a problem with either of you wankers," Kyle said, and the three of them laughed. "All I want to do is sing with you guys and write. I don't care who sings the lead on my songs."

"I'm cool with that," Zander said. "I guess I can give up the spotlight sometimes, too."

"And I won't tease you guys so much," Heath said, and fist-bumped them both.

"So you guys promise not to fight over this silly PS contest?" Jilly asked, speaking in a voice she probably uses with her brother. "Let my dad pick the winner, and just stay out of it. Tell the label publicists you like all the entries—except that stupid Sabrina one. I mean, a poster for a school dance compared to a charity concert or building a house? Lame."

I tried not to laugh, but I couldn't help it. The laugh came out all nervous and sounded like a sick sea lion. I could have sworn I saw Kyle look my way, but I pretended not to notice.

"Deal," they all agreed. Then they stood up and hugged.

Jilly sounded chipper. "I'll tell Daddy and Piper the good news. Perfect Storm is back!"

"Were we ever really gone?" Kyle asked the other two as they started to leave. Mikey G. stopped blocking the door. "You guys want to go get some grub and talk tunes?"

"Sounds good," Heath said, and the three of them walked out.

Jilly threw her arm around me. "You saved PS! Daddy is going to love you."

I watched the three boys disappear into the hallway. They were talking a mile a minute. "It was a group effort," I told her, but secretly I was pretty pleased with myself.

PS was going to make it another day, and I had had something to do with it!

Ladies and gentleman, we are here today to thank the girl group MAC ATTACK for saving PERFECT STORM from ROBOTIC MOMINATOR, one of the world's most-wanted villains.

Earlier this week, MAC ATTACK learned that ROBOTIC MOMINATOR was preparing to destroy PS. They not only stopped the plan in its tracks, they also captured ROBOTIC MOMINATOR!

WOOOO

As a thank-you for saving the world—and our favorite band—we'd like to present them with this key to the city and ask them to say a few words.

MAYOR'S PODIUM

Thank you, everyone. We just did what any Perfect Storm fan would do.

Don't be modest, Mac. The plan to save the band was your idea!

And the city hasn't heard the best part yet—tell them about the concert!

To make up for the damage we caused to a few city buildings in our attempt to capture ROBOTIC MOMINATOR...

The Capitol Records building needed an update, anyway!

We have teamed up with Perfect Storm to give the city the best concert they've ever seen!

And remember—no matter what the peril is, Mac Attack will always be there to save the day!

## Wednesday, March 23

### LOCATION: Los Angeles, California

I did not win a key to Los Angeles as Mac Attack did in my comic. I tried not to be disappointed. When Mom showed up, I asked her if anyone in the press had mentioned me single-handedly saving the band. She just laughed.

"Mac," she said, holding me close and stroking my hair like she did when I was little and there was a thunderstorm. We were sitting on the couch in our room while my friends continued to snooze. We had been up pretty late celebrating with ice cream again last night.
"Rule number one

about pop stars—the only person they ever credit is themselves." I didn't say anything. It was a bit of a bummer. "But don't you worry—Briggs and I know what you and the girls did, and maybe someday they'll write songs about you." She winked. "In fact, I think one of them already did."

My cheeks flushed. Did Mom know I had a crush on Kyle? Or did she think I still liked Zander?

Mom slapped her thigh. "I forgot to ask you. Did you see that a Sabrina from New York made the finalists? Is that your friend?"

It was time to fess up. I told Mom how I had written Zander the poem and drawn the picture before I knew I had any chance of actually meeting him. I had used my middle name because I was afraid she would be mad that I was asking a boy to the dance (the no-dating-till-high-school thing). I'd had no idea we'd wind up on the road with Perfect Storm and my poster would wind up being chosen as a finalist in a PS contest.

Now that I knew the guys, Zander felt more like a friend, Heath more like a brother, and . . . well, I left Kyle out of it. I started to get a bit hysterical and choked up at the end when I told Mom how I didn't want the guys to know Sabrina was me. Mom listened without interrupting—her tour manager training made her good at that—and then she hugged me tighter.

"One question: You're sure you don't want to go to your dance with Zander anymore?"

I shook my head slowly. "Zander would make a fun brother—well, not as fun as Heath—but as far as a husband I could live on a Caribbean island with and sell my art? No. Way."

Mom laughed. "I knew you were a smart girl. And you're right—there is no dating till high school. You're way too young," she said sharply, "but there is no reason why you can't have an escort to your first middle school dance."

"Really?" I said softly. I had worried for nothing. My mom really was cool.

303

"Is there someone you *do* want to go to the dance with?" Mom pried.

Kyle. I wanted to go with Kyle.

I wasn't ready to admit that out loud yet.

"Maybe," I said.

"Well, either way you're in luck. Family members of personnel who work for the band are not allowed to enter the contest, so that means you're off the hook. I'll tell Briggs that I got a call from Sabrina's mom, and she wants her daughter to pull out of the contest," Mom said. "I'll cite security reasons or something like that." She patted my hand. "I'll take care of it."

I hugged her. "Thanks, Mom."

"Publicity has already spun a reason behind the band's spat—lack of sleep, they were just joking, et cetera—and they prepared a press statement about them staying on Lemon Ade's tour and announcing the contest winner on Z100. Things are looking up again." Mom smiled. "Can you believe that soon we'll be home for a few days? And just in time for your dance, too."

Home. Suddenly I missed it. My bed, my PS posters. Cody the dog barking next door. It would be good to be home for a *few* days. Wait. Just a few days? "You mean we're going back out on tour?"

Mom laughed. "Yes, we're part of the band for the foreseeable future. Are you up for road life and tutoring with Krissy and the boys' shenanigans?"

"Definitely!" I jumped up and prepared to wake Iris and Scarlet. I felt a hundred pounds lighter, which would make me zero pounds, but that's beside the point.

"Oh, and Mac?" Mom's voice was suddenly sterner. "Try to find a way to celebrate today without ordering another ice-cream sundae bar, okay? Room service adds up quick."

I swallowed hard. "Okay." The truth was I didn't need ice cream to be happy. I didn't need to wake Iris and Scarlet at the moment, either. Let them sleep. I'd run and find Jilly for now.

I rushed out of the room and ran smack into Kyle.

I went down flat like a pancake.

"Are you okay?" Kyle helped me up. I felt slightly stunned, and not just because Kyle had on jeans and a red hoodie and looked like a guy who belonged on a magazine cover (which I guess he was). "You are kind of klutzy."

"I am," I said with a nervous laugh.

"Well, I was coming to give you this." Kyle held out a sheet of paper. "I'm sorry it's taken forever for me to finish it. I've been a little sidetracked."

I looked down at the paper. "The Story of a Girl," by Kyle Beyer. It was a song. A song Kyle wrote for me!

"Don't read it in front of me," Kyle said quickly. "You'll give me a serious case of the collywobbles." I looked at him strangely. "You'll make me nervous," he translated.

"Oh, okay," I said, feeling very collywobbles myself.

"Catch you later," Kyle said, and began walking down the hall.

Who was he kidding? There was no way I was waiting till he was gone to read the lyrics.

### *"The Story of a Girl," by Kyle Beyer*

*See her standing there in her messed-up*
    *kicks,*
*Looking like she's got the whole world to*
    *fix,*
*With a smile that feels like a million watts*
*And a laugh that makes me want to rock.*
*Oh! . . . She's a superhero in training,*
*I'll be forever waiting.*

307

(Chorus)

*This is the story of a girl,*

*A girl who makes you want to whirl,*

*A girl who makes you feel like you're miles*
*   from shore*

*And you don't want for anything more.*

*This is the story of a girl.*

The Story of a Girl
by Kyle Beyer

See her standing there in her messed-up kicks
Looking like she's got
The whole world to fix
With a smile that feels like a million watts
And a laugh that makes me want to rock!
Oh! She's a superhero in training
I'll be forever waiting...

This song was about ME? Did Kyle maybe, sort of, possibly, kind of have a crush on me, too? If he did, then he'd definitely . . .

"Kyle!" I yelled down the hall. When he didn't turn right away, I ran after him.

He turned around. "You read the lyrics already, didn't you?"

I took a deep breath. "Yes, and there's something I have to ask you."

LOCATION: HOME! Long Island, New York, it's a heck of a town!

"How are you doing, Brookside Middle School!" the DJ yelled into his mic.

He got a lackluster cheer in return. He was clearly no Lemon Ade or PS.

Okay, sure, the school dance was held in the school gym, which still smelled slightly like twice-worn socks, the food was soggy heroes and bright red punch that could ruin your dress with one splash, and the decorations were some balloons and paper stars hanging from the basketball nets around the court, but to me it was the most beautiful gym in the world.

Kyle Beyer had agreed to go to my middle school dance with me!

Yep, I had been brave in that hotel hallway. I channeled my inner Mac Attack without a nail file or a velvet rope to climb down a building with and blurted out the words to Kyle that I had been holding in for so long:

"Dance, me, go, school, with, music, tie, cute in suit?" The words came out garbled, and I laughed loud like a hyena.

Kyle blinked.

I tried again. "What I meant to say was, if you weren't busy, and you were in New York when this was happening, would you, could you, maybe want to go to my school dance with me?"

Kyle broke into a grin. "I've never been to a school dance before. Sounds brilliant."

And now, a few weeks later, here we were. No one dresses too fancy for these things, but Mom had still gotten me a new dress while we were on the road that was as blue as Captain America's suit (I considered that good luck), and Kyle was wearing jeans with a suit jacket and a skinny tie because that was very pop star of him.

"Do you think we ought to try to dance because we're at a dance?" Kyle asked me. We had been standing on the side of the gym talking to fans and Iris, Scarlet, and Jilly since we arrived an hour earlier. Iris and Scarlet had decided the middle school date curse was a bunch of garbage and had instead gone solo—technically. They had brought Jilly, so really they were a trio.

I laughed nervously. "Yeah, but this is a slow song."

"So?" Kyle said.

Jilly, Iris, and Scarlet looked like they were trying to catch flies. I nearly bit my tongue. "Okay," I said, and walked with him out to the middle of the dance floor. Mikey G. followed so people would give us some room. Kyle had quite the group of followers.

Kyle ran a hand through his hair and sort of

313

laughed. "Okay, I don't have a clue what we do next! I've never really slow-danced with a girl before."

"Me neither," I said, blushing. "I mean, maybe we just . . ." I placed Kyle's hands around my waist. I put my hands on his shoulders and felt

a little loopy. I'd seen people do this in movies, but this was awkward in real life! I giggled nervously as we started to sway.

"Dance teacher, comic-book creator, and band-breakup stopper," Kyle said. "Is there anything you can't do, Mackenzie Lowell?"

"Nope." I was blushing so hard I couldn't think of anything better to say, not when Kyle was this close and staring at me.

"Did you hear we picked the contest winner on Z100 today?" Kyle asked.

PS had been on the morning show with Elvis Duran that day. Mom said it was a huge hit (I, unfortunately, had to go to actual school, which was the downside of being back in New York for a few days). Apparently, some girl even fainted outside the studio and had to be taken away in an ambulance! This week alone Perfect Storm's Twitter followers had topped one million, and their YouTube channel subscribers were even higher. Mom said it hadn't been officially announced yet, but it looked like Perfect Storm was getting their own headlining tour, and guess who gets to go on the road with them for it? ME!

"We're going with the girl from Habitat for Humanity."

"I really liked that one," I said. "That girl deserved to win."

"It's a shame about that Sabrina entry, though," Kyle said, and for some reason his face looked a little funny. "Too bad her mom made her pull out of the contest. Zander really wanted her to win so he could go to that dance with her. Her drawing of the group was aces, wasn't it?"

Did Kyle know I was Sabrina? Had he figured out I drew that picture? I could hear a swishing sound in my ears. Was that a new song playing or my heart thumping in my chest? I wasn't going to tell Kyle if he wasn't going to ask me. "Yeah, her drawing *was* aces," I said carefully, stealing Kyle's favorite phrase, "but maybe she decided she wanted her drawing to be aces for someone else." I was starting to ramble. "Maybe she sent that poster in before she knew there was a contest. Before she knew enough about Perfect Storm to figure out who she really wanted to take to her school dance. Maybe she realized who she really liked was you."

I was breathing heavily. Kyle and I just looked at each other. We had stopped swaying and were just standing in the middle of the dance floor.

"You think so?" Kyle asked quietly.

"Maybe." I felt my heartbeat slow down again. "People change their minds."

Kyle grinned. "I hope you're right."

"Hey, you two!" Heath yelled from the stage. "Could you stop dancing so we could perform some songs? The natives are getting a little restless."

"Will you excuse me?" Kyle asked politely.

"Of course," I said, and watched Kyle run off to join the guys onstage.

317

Yep. Perfect Storm had agreed to perform at the Brookside Middle School dance. Briggs thought it would be great with the local press, and publicity agreed. I think it also gave Mom an excuse to keep an eye on me, but at least she hadn't come over and actually tried to dance with us yet.

"What were you two just talking about?" Iris

asked when she and Scarlet ran over. I heard Kyle tuning up his guitar onstage.

"How are you doing, Brookside Middle School?" Zander shouted, and my classmates screamed (much louder than they had for the DJ).

"He didn't try to kiss you, did he?" Scarlet sounded frantic. "When he was standing so close like that, I was sure he was going to try to kiss you!"

I shook my head. I wasn't sure I even wanted Kyle to kiss me. Right now, at least. I mean, I was only twelve, and I had a comic book to finish and album covers to design and the rest of seventh grade to worry about. And Kyle was a soon-to-be international pop star.

We both had a lot going on, and I was just happy to have him come to the dance.

"Nope!" I said.

But that didn't mean I couldn't daydream about the day it would happen and our future after that.

I'm thinking about a life in Paris. There's a lot of famous art there for Kyle and me to check out. He'll be part of the biggest band on the planet, and I'll be his album-cover/comic-book-designing wife. The possibilities are endless.

But first there is a Perfect Storm tour to plan! I can't wait to see what happens on the road with the boys next.

# ACKNOWLEDGMENTS

As a girl who grew up in a room bursting with New Kids on the Block posters and a Joey McIntrye pillowcase, getting the chance to write about a girl who goes on the road with her favorite boy band is a dream. Thank you to Little, Brown Books for Young Readers for letting me write this lucky thirteenth novel with them. It wouldn't have been possible without my fearless editor, Pam Gruber. I feel so lucky to work with someone who equally enjoys talking about comic books and ballet flats. Shout-outs to the rest of the hardworking LBYR team, including Andrew Smith; Melanie Chang; my fierce publicist, Kristina Aven; Leslie Shumate; Tracy Shaw; Wendy Dopkin; and Erica Stahler.

This is the first time I've ever had the pleasure of working on a book with illustrations, and Kristen Gudsnuk made the experience a dream. Kristen, you captured Perfect Storm and Mac in a way I never could have imagined. (And your comic-book illustrations rock. Mac Attack would definitely approve!)

To Dan Mandel, my agent: You truly are Dan the Man. Thanks for always believing in me and my projects. I feel so fortunate to have you on my side.

Writing is so much more fun when you have friends to share ideas with. Thanks to the biggest boy band lover I know, Elizabeth Eulberg, for giving this book a first read. Thanks also go to Julia DeVillers for all the middle grade notes, Kieran Scott for always having the best advice a friend could ask for, and Katie Sise, Jennifer E. Smith, Sarah Mylnowski, Tiffany Schmidt, and Courtney Sheinmel for being on this journey with me.

To The Dance Place competition dancers (and owner and friend Miana DeLucia) in North Bellmore, New York—thank you for letting me storm practices to pick your brains about why you love boy bands like One Direction. You are my kind of girls.

To Mike, Tyler, Dylan, (and, of course, Jack), thank you for putting up with the crazy schedule, the odd writing hours, and the months when I've been talking so much on school visits, I lose my voice (I secretly think you all may enjoy this). Thank you for inspiring me and making me laugh every day.

And finally to my awesome, inspiring readers. Thank you for all your notes, e-mails, and comments about my books. I feel so lucky to get to write stories you enjoy reading. Mac is as close as I've ever come to putting a character like me on the page. For your enjoyment, I'll also tell you this—I just may have written a poem to New Kids on the Block back in the day that reads a lot like the one Mac wrote. This is why I always say it never hurts to put yourself out there: I got an actual reply, which I have kept to this day. The journey is what you make of it. Make yours a great one.

# Want more
# MAC ATTACK and PERFECT STORM?

Continue reading for a sneak peek at
*VIP: Battle of the Bands,*
the sequel to *VIP: I'm With the Band.*

Available now.

**LOCATION: SoundEscape Recording Studio—New York City**

I, Mackenzie Sabrina Lowell, do solemnly swear on Perfect Storm's potential world music domination that everything I write in this journal is the truth, starting with this:

I'M IN A RECORDING STUDIO LISTENING TO PERFECT STORM RECORD THEIR FIRST FULL-LENGTH ALBUM!

Me!

I'd pinch myself to make sure I'm not dreaming, but then I'd wind up with a welt that turns black and blue and forces me to wear a jacket in May. Instead, I make lists.

## MAC'S TOP FIVE REASONS WHY THIS IS GOING TO BE THE BEST SUMMER EVER:

1. Mom is taking me back out on the road with Perfect Storm when school ends. Since it'll be my summer break, that means no Krissy tutoring sessions! YES!

2. No school also means Scarlet and Iris can come with Jilly and me to some of the tour stops. (Iris says this can only happen if she and Scarlet pool their babysitting money and stop buying PS shirts, but my fingers and toes are crossed!)

3. Being on the road means steering clear of Jones Beach. Mom usually drags me there at least twice a week in the summer, even though we all know the ocean has sharks. But there'll be no time for the beach when we're on tour, so I'm saved from a possible shark attack for another year! YAY!

4. Extra time on the tour bus means more time for me to finish my *Mac Attack* comic book! I've already got a third of it done from our last road trip. This time there'll be no annoying distractions (like essays on the generals of the American Revolution. Yawn) to keep me from my artistic dreams.

5. Touring with Perfect Storm means I get to spend more time with my crush, Kyle Beyer! Let me write that glorious name a few more times: KyleBeyerKyleBeyerKyleBeyer. Sigh... I could say his name all day! It's *that* dreamy. Just like Kyle!

"COO-COO-CA-CHEW!"

My pen with the fuzzy pink monster topper drew a long, jittery line at the sound of the bizarre birdcall. I'd been hearing that sound over and over all afternoon.

"CAW! CAW! CAW!" Perfect Storm's producer, The Raven, crowed again with full-on bird flaps to emphasize his excitement. His birdcall was so loud that I thought the glass window separating us from the band was going to shatter into a million pieces.

That's exactly what happened in *The Sharkinator*

*Returns*. My friends and I watched it during a sleepover last night even though Mom begged us not to. In *The Sharkinator Returns*, though, the glass in an aquarium shattered and the sharks attacked a group of high school kids on a field trip and... and...I think I blacked out after that.

"Is this guy serious with the bird bit?" Scarlet whispered to Iris and Jilly.

"It's so annoying," Jilly agreed. Her dad is Perfect Storm's manager, so she's met a lot of music producers, but I was pretty sure The Raven had to be the strangest yet. "And you thought Einstein was weird with all his 'scientific formulas' for making a hit song."

Jilly said bands like Perfect Storm work with a lot of different producers when they're doing an album, but I was starting to miss Einstein and his crazy beats. He had a weird name, but he looked normal and stuck to human language. The Raven looked like a bird with his black hair, big nose, and wiry, thin body; and the twenty-one-year-old was even dressed head to toe in black like, well, a raven. I wasn't sure ravens crowed, though. Didn't they just hang out around cemeteries and look scary?

"Perfect Storm's tracks are blowing the roof off this joint!" The Raven said to Jilly's dad. "This bird hears a number one single!"

Suddenly, I felt an overwhelming sense of pride. PS was killing it in this studio session and had been working for ten hours straight (I'd only been here for two). Inspired, I let out a bird-call of my own, even though I'd never made a sound like that in my life.

"CA-CAW! PS RULES!" I cheered. There was silence. Then I heard PS laughing through the speakers. I quickly sat back down as The Raven gave me his best evil-villain glare. "Sorry. I got carried away."

"I am the only one who speaks during recording sessions," The Raven said stiffly. "I need silence to reflect on the band's energy."

I leaned closer to the girls, squeezing Scarlet against the padded walls. "It won't happen again," I whispered. I already knew The Raven didn't like us "Storm Chasers" being there, but that was TOO BAD. We were invited!

"The girls are just excited," said my mom.

Or as I now refer to her: THE COOLEST MOM IN THE ENTIRE UNIVERSE (even the parts that aren't discovered yet). And here's why: A few months ago, my mom gave up her desk job to become Perfect Storm's tour manager, and she took me along for the ride.

"Understood, but absolute silence is key in a recording studio," said The Raven. "My baby birds are learning to fly in there. This is not really a place meant for children."

"Hey, Mac!" I heard my name amplified through the sound system before I could complain about being called a child. Heath Holland was grinning and waving at me through the glass. "We're really digging that birdcall you just made," he said. "Think you could record the sound for us to use on our song 'The Story of a Girl'? It's going to be the first single off our new album."

The Raven frowned. "I really don't think it's strong enough for a single. As I've said before, my pick is definitely 'Bring Back the Sun.' I co-wrote it and…"

The Raven was ruining my moment! "I'll record the sound!" I stood up, pushed my way past the girls, my mom, and Briggs to reach the bendy microphone that The Raven was holding and practically yanked it out of his hands.

"Great," said Zander Welling from inside the studio booth, on the other side of the glass. He ran a hand through his wavy curls that were always falling in front of his electric blue eyes. "The caw sounds like a girl's scream, like the kind we hear at concerts. But make it louder, with more feeling, this time."

"Um, Mac?" Jilly said quietly. Whatever she wanted could wait. PS needed me!

"Add in some different bird sounds, too," Heath suggested. "Maybe an ostrich or a pterodactyl?"

"A pterodactyl?" Zander repeated.

"Yeah," Heath said pointedly. "The dinosaur bird thingie. Go for it, Mac."

I looked back at my friends triumphantly. Jilly was mouthing something, but I closed

my eyes and took a deep breath. "COO-COO-CAWWWWWWWWW! SCREECH!" I added The Raven's bird-wing flap for effect.

Heath and Zander applauded, but the person I most wanted a reaction from was holding his head like he had a headache.

Kyle, Perfect Storm's sensitive British guitarist and now songwriter—aka my *current* crush and seventh-grade Spring Fling date—was staring at me. His soulful brown eyes make me envision a future in Paris together. I'll write comic books in an apartment with a view of the Eiffel Tower while Kyle sits at the other end of our shared desk and writes awesome songs that are about me and a life filled with lots of berets and amazing cheeses. (Jilly says Paris is all about cheese.)

"NICE!" said Heath. "That caw is the techno vibe we've been missing!"

"I'm confused," The Raven said. "What's happening?"

Briggs leaned over and spoke into my mic.

"Boys, I think you're getting a little loopy from all that time in stale air. Maybe we should take a break."

"After Mac records the sound, Briggsy." Heath grabbed a green guitar the same shade as his current hair color and motioned for me to come into the recording booth. He strummed the strings and hummed my caw sound. Zander joined in. "Now your turn, Mac!" I watched Zander hold up his iPhone and point it directly at me to record.

Kyle jumped up. "Don't do it!" Heath and Zander groaned. "They're trying to make you the victim of their latest YouTube video."

OH. My face heated up like I'd spent too long in a hotel hot tub. I was seconds away from being a YouTube joke called Bird Girl. "Ha!" I laughed weakly. "Almost got me." I backed away from the glass as Kyle gave me a sympathetic nod.

"It would have been perfect," Heath moaned. "She was flapping her wings and everything."

He demonstrated, and I could see that his arms were covered in new fake-tattoo sleeves.

"Break time!" Briggs announced, and The Raven threw down his notes and left the room. "Take fifteen and then we'll try to finish this song within the hour. You guys have an early morning tomorrow with that Z100 interview."

The boys went out the back of the recording studio, while my mom and Briggs walked off talking about all the tour stuff they had to get done before we went back out on the road again.

My friends were sympathetic. Iris pulled me in for a hug. Her reddish-blond hair smelled like strawberries. "The guys like you enough to prank you and let the whole world watch! That has to be a good thing."

"I wish Heath pranked me," Scarlet said, looking longingly at the recording booth that was now empty. Her expression quickly turned sour. "Not that I ever would have fallen for that joke. Seriously, Mac. I thought you knew the guys better than that."

Scarlet has never been one to sugarcoat things like Iris.

"I tried to warn you." Jilly jumped into The Raven's now-vacant producer's chair and gave it a spin. "Didn't you see me mouth 'Don't do it'?"

"I thought you were saying 'YES, do it'!" I grumbled. "Now I've humiliated myself in front of Kyle by flapping like Big Bird."

"I don't think Big Bird actually flaps," Iris pointed out. "Doesn't he have really small wings?"

"He's way too big to fly," Scarlet agreed. "He'd never lift off the ground."

I was still huffy. "My point is, I looked ridiculous instead of cool and fun like I was at the Spring Fling."

"Not the Spring Fling recap again!" Scarlet slapped her head, and I noticed that her black and gray nails looked exactly like Heath's. He loved to borrow our nail polish and paint his nails funky colors. "Mac, we love you, but how many times are we going to do the play-by-play?"

Okay, so maybe I typed up a minute-by-minute report of Kyle's and my time at the dance together and pulled it out every few days to recap it again. (Example: 6:57 PM KYLE: *Wow, this gym is a scorcher! Is the heat on in here?* ME: *No, it's always this hot.*) Was it a bit much? Maybe. But can I help it if I like reliving the single greatest night of my life? "You guys don't know what I was going to say," I complained.

Jilly pulled her gum out of her mouth and raised her hand like we were in the middle of a school session with Krissy, who's in Los Angeles for the summer tutoring a Disney Channel star instead of us. "You guys had so much fun, but you've become good friends and you don't want to ruin that by Kyle thinking you want to be more than friends…"

"If your mom wants to ruin your life by saying you're too young to date your future husband, then it's pointless to even think about having a boyfriend...," Scarlet added.

"But when you're older, you can totally see the two of you settling in Paris and eating croissants every day...," Iris finished.

"Ooh! Ooh!" Scarlet started jumping around. "You know what Mac hasn't brought up today? How Kyle wrote her—"

"—A SONG," the three of them said in unison.

I was getting annoyed now. "Can I help it if I'm excited the boy I want to move to Paris with wrote a song about me? I mean, if Kyle didn't like me, he wouldn't have written me a song. Right?"

"YES!" the girls said in unison again.

"Whoops-a-daisy!" someone said in a British accent I knew all too well. "I'll come back later."

I slowly turned around.

Oh no. Oh no. Oh no. Oh no.

I felt like I swallowed a surfboard (which a shark did on *The Sharkinator Returns* last night. It wasn't pretty).

Kyle was standing behind us, and I had a feeling he'd heard every word I had just said.

**JEN CALONITA** is bummed she never got to go on the road with her favorite boy band growing up (New Kids on the Block), but she did eventually get to interview one of the band members when she became an entertainment editor. She's also interviewed stars like Justin Timberlake and Beyoncé. Jen is the author of the Secrets of My Hollywood Life and Fairy Tale Reform School series. She currently lives in New York with her husband, Mike; sons, Dylan and Tyler; and their Chihuahua, Captain Jack Sparrow. She'd love to hear what bands you love! You can visit her online at jencalonitaonline.com.

**KRISTEN GUDSNUK** is the creator of the comic *Henchgirl*. She lives in New York City.